Titus
Andronicus

by

WILLIAM
SHAKESPEARE

WSP

WASHINGTON SQUARE PRESS
PUBLISHED BY POCKET BOOKS
New York   London   Toronto   Sydney   Tokyo   Singapore

Most Washington Square Press Books are available at special quantity discounts for bulk purchases for sales promotions, premiums or fund raising. Special books or book excerpts can also be created to fit specific needs.

For details write the office of the Vice President of Special Markets, Pocket Books, 1230 Avenue of the Americas, New York, New York 10020.

A Washington Square Press Publication of
POCKET BOOKS, a division of Simon & Schuster, Inc.
1230 Avenue of the Americas, New York, N.Y. 10020

Copyright © 1967 by Simon & Schuster, Inc.

All rights reserved, including the right to reproduce
this book or portions thereof in any form whatsoever.
For information address Pocket Books, 1230 Avenue
of the Americas, New York, N.Y. 10020

ISBN: 0-671-66915-X

First Pocket Books printing March 1968

10   9   8   7   6   5

WASHINGTON SQUARE PRESS and WSP colophon are
registered trademarks of Simon & Schuster, Inc.

Printed in the U.S.A.

This edition of *Titus Andronicus* is designed to provide a readable text of one of Shakespeare's early works, a typical Elizabethan medley of blood and horror. In the centuries since Shakespeare, many changes have occurred in the meanings of words, and some clarification of Shakespeare's vocabulary may be helpful. To provide the reader with necessary notes in the most accessible format, we have placed them on the pages facing the text that they explain. We have tried to make them as brief and simple as possible. Preliminary to the text we have also included a brief statement of essential information about Shakespeare and his stage. Readers desiring more detailed information should refer to the books suggested in the references, and if still further information is needed, the bibliographies in those books will provide the necessary clues to the literature of the subject.

The early texts of Shakespeare's plays provide only scattered stage directions and no indications of setting, and it is conventional for modern editors to add these to clarify the action. Such additions, and additions to entrances and exits, as well as many indications of act and scene divisions, are placed in square brackets.

All illustrations are from material in the Folger Library collections.

L. B. W.

V. A. L.

April 15, 1967

Popular Horror Play

Because of its sensationalism, bloodshed, and horrors, sentimental idolaters of Shakespeare have long tried to absolve him from the authorship of *Titus Andronicus*. They forget that William Shakespeare was first of all a man of the theatre, even from his earliest days, and that he was intent upon writing a theatrical success rather than a pretty piece to read in the study or the drawing room. Furthermore, the sentimentalists also forget that *Titus Andronicus* in its own day was a rousing success, both as a stage play and as a book to be read. This was a work of Shakespeare's youthful apprenticeship, and it proved to his contemporaries in the theatre that he could be trusted to turn out an effective drama that would gain an audience.

This play has puzzled scholars and stimulated a great deal of speculation about its authorship, its date, and its sources. Some earlier scholars, admitting that Shakespeare clearly had a hand in the composition of *Titus Andronicus*, attempted to show that he merely collaborated in the revision of an old play and that portions of the drama as it survives were the handiwork of someone else, possibly George Peele. Several modern scholars now assign the entire play to Shakespeare, though admitting that differences in style can be discerned; for example, Act I is more pedestrian and less poetic than Act II. But stylistic differences, especially in apprentice work, can prove very little. The young playwright may have been experimenting, or perhaps he just warmed to his work by Act II. Francis Meres, in *Palladis Tamia* (1598), named Shakespeare as the author of *Titus Andronicus*, and the editors of the First Folio of 1623, who were Shakespeare's colleagues and in a position to know, included it. Sensational as it is, the evidence points to Shakespeare's responsibility in its composition.

The date of the first performance of the play is uncertain. An allusion to *Titus Andronicus* occurs in an old play, *A Knack to Know a Knave*, acted in 1592 and printed in 1594. The unique First Quarto of *Titus Andronicus*, preserved in the Folger Library, was printed in 1594 and was described on the title page as "Plaide by the Right Honourable the Earle of Darbie, Earle of Pembrooke, and Earle of Sussex their Seruants." This would seem to indicate that the play had been on the stage for some time before its printing. It may have been performed in 1592 or 1593, although some scholars have tried to push the date back as far as 1589. Clearly, it is one of Shakespeare's early efforts in dramatic writing.

The sources of the play are also uncertain. Although it falls roughly in the class of "Roman plays," it does not fit into any recorded Roman history. The characters and incidents are fictional. Some evidence points to the possibility that Shakespeare may have reworked an old play, which was probably based on a forgotten romance. In recent years an eighteenth-century prose narrative, *The History of Titus Andronicus*, has turned up in the Folger Library. Some scholars profess to see in this narrative, which they think derives from a sixteenth-century original, a source for the play, but their contention is merely conjectural. The most obvious source for situations in *Titus Andronicus* is found in Ovid's *Metamorphoses*, particularly the tale of Philomela in Book VI, which parallels the rape and mutilation of Lavinia. Other parallel incidents occur elsewhere in Ovid, the classical poet that Shakespeare probably read as a schoolboy and knew best. The characterization of the wicked Moor was conventional in Elizabethan and earlier literature. References to detailed discussions of Shakespeare's sources will be found in the reading list at the end of this introduction.

Sensationalism like that of *Titus Andronicus* was popular with Elizabethan audiences, not merely with the groundlings of the public theatres but with university audiences as well. The plays of the Roman dramatist Seneca were well known and exerted a powerful influence on early Elizabethan drama. Tragic sensationalism was a characteristic of Senecan drama, and Shakespeare could have found a suggestion for the cannibal feast in Seneca's *Thyestes*, where Atreus murders his brother's sons and, acting as cook, serves them up. Other suggestions may also have come from Seneca and Senecan adaptations on the stage before Shakespeare wrote his play.

Nothing could be too bloody and horrible for an Elizabethan audience. Thomas Kyd had written a sensational play in *The Spanish Tragedy*, first performed about 1586 and many times thereafter to become perhaps the most popular drama of the age. It has murders and hangings on stage, with the appearance of ghosts and the abstraction Revenge. *The Spanish Tragedy* set the pattern for the revenge tragedy, which Shakespeare imperfectly adapted in *Titus Andronicus* and carried to masterful perfection in *Hamlet*.

Christopher Marlowe, from whom Shakespeare learned something about stage techniques as well as the pattern of his blank verse, delighted audiences with sensations. *Tamburlaine* (1587) provides fighting on stage, murders, and two characters who brain themselves against the cages in which they are imprisoned. *The Jew of Malta* (ca. 1589) in the character Barabas shows a villain almost as deep-dyed as Aaron in *Titus Andronicus*, and in the end he is hanged before being dropped into a boiling cauldron on stage.

Other playwrights were equally lacking in squeamishness. Executions, murders, mutilations, and rapes were part of the common dramatic fare. Sometimes executions and mutilations called upon the juggler's art and supplied realistic detail, with blood flowing on the stage. A character could be flayed alive with a false skin, and a "bladder of vinegar" or red wine would make the scene sufficiently gory.

Our own age need feel no superiority over the Elizabethans because of their appetite for gruesome horrors. Our own television programs exhibit mayhem and slaughter sufficient to make any Elizabethan stage manager envious. The New York and London stages find no horror too terrible, and Tennessee Williams even shows that cannibalism is not unsuitable for our stage. On the London stage a play entertained its audience with the stoning to death of a baby. Peter Weiss, in *The Persecution and Assassination of Jean-Paul Marat as Performed by the Inmates of the Asylum of Charenton under the Direction of the Marquis de Sade*, has recently written a stage success that audiences appear to savor and relish. Horror plays, horror movies, horror television, and "sick" entertainment flourish as never before.

Shakespeare demonstrated that he could take the pulse of the public and give them precisely what they wanted in *Titus Andronicus*. How many times the play was performed in the author's lifetime, we do not know, but evidence points to continuing popularity. First printed in 1594, it had later quarto editions in 1600 (a reprint of the First Quarto) and 1611 (a reprint of the Second Quarto). The Folio version of 1623 was printed from a playhouse copy of Quarto 3 and added Scene ii in Act III, which does not appear in any of the quarto editions. The present edition is based on the First Quarto, with corrections and emendations suggested by the later versions.

Titus Andronicus had frequent revivals during the first half of the seventeenth century. Versions of the play also were frequently performed in Germany and Holland, where its horrors made it a favorite. Shakespeare's original play may have been taken to the Continent by English actors. At the Restoration, after the reopening of the theatres, which had been closed in 1642 by the Puritans, *Titus* was not one of Shakespeare's plays chosen for immediate revival. Eventually, however, it appeared in 1678 in an adaptation made by Edward Ravenscroft, which he called *Titus Andronicus, or the Rape of Lavinia*. In the printed version of this adaptation, Ravenscroft first questioned Shakespeare's authorship by stating that he had been told that Shakespeare "only gave some Master-touches to one or two of the Principal Parts or Characters; this I am apt to believe because 'tis the most incorrect and indigested piece in all his Works. It seems rather a heap of Rubbish than a Structure." Since Ravenscroft was condemning the earlier play in order to enhance interest in his own version, and was merely repeating vague hearsay about the authorship, scholars of the present day do not give his words much credence.

During the eighteenth century *Titus Andronicus*

was acted at intervals, and in the nineteenth century the Negro actor Ira Aldridge made a great hit in the part of Aaron. It has been acted from time to time ever since. The most successful performance in modern times was that directed in London and on the Continent in 1957 by Sir Laurence Olivier. Spectators who went expecting to be bored with an Elizabethan blood-and-thunder play remained to be fascinated, if not by Shakespeare's writing, at least by his theatricality and the interpretation given it by good actors. Not every critic, however, agreed that it was a notable drama. When it was received with enthusiasm in Paris, one London reviewer observed that its reception there merely proved that the French never really understood or appreciated the true Shakespeare.

Few indeed are the critics who will defend *Titus Andronicus* as a great play or one that adds to the stature of its author. Hereward T. Price, however, who spent many years studying it and preparing a Variorum edition which he did not live to finish, always maintained that it had many excellences. He emphasized its vigorous language, its occasional passages of genuine poetic inspiration, and its perception of the demands of the playhouse. Shakespeare, he insisted, had studied his craft exceptionally well and had written a play that foreshadowed his great tragedies.

THE AUTHOR

As early as 1598 Shakespeare was so well known as a literary and dramatic craftsman that Francis Meres, in his *Palladis Tamia: Wits Treasury*, referred in flattering terms to him as "mellifluous and honey-tongued Shakespeare," famous for his *Venus and Adonis*, his *Lucrece*, and "his sugared sonnets," which were circulating "among his private friends." Meres observes further that "as Plautus and Seneca are accounted the best for comedy and tragedy among the Latins, so Shakespeare among the English is the most excellent in both kinds for the stage," and he mentions a dozen plays that had made a name for Shakespeare. He concludes with the remark that "the Muses would speak with Shakespeare's fine filed phrase if they would speak English."

To those acquainted with the history of the Elizabethan and Jacobean periods, it is incredible that anyone should be so naïve or ignorant as to doubt the reality of Shakespeare as the author of the plays that bear his name. Yet so much nonsense has been written about other "candidates" for the plays that it is well to remind readers that no credible evidence that would stand up in a court of law has ever been adduced to prove either that Shakespeare did not write his plays or that anyone else wrote them. All the theories offered for the authorship of

Francis Bacon, the Earl of Derby, the Earl of Oxford, the Earl of Hertford, Christopher Marlowe, and a score of other candidates are mere conjectures spun from the active imaginations of persons who confuse hypothesis and conjecture with evidence.

As Meres' statement of 1598 indicates, Shakespeare was already a popular playwright whose name carried weight at the box office. The obvious reputation of Shakespeare as early as 1598 makes the effort to prove him a myth one of the most absurd in the history of human perversity.

The anti-Shakespeareans talk darkly about a plot of vested interests to maintain the authorship of Shakespeare. Nobody has any vested interest in Shakespeare, but every scholar is interested in the truth and in the quality of evidence advanced by special pleaders who set forth hypotheses in place of facts.

The anti-Shakespeareans base their arguments upon a few simple premises, all of them false. These false premises are that Shakespeare was an unlettered yokel without any schooling, that nothing is known about Shakespeare, and that only a noble lord or the equivalent in background could have written the plays. The facts are that more is known about Shakespeare than about most dramatists of his day, that he had a very good education, acquired in the Stratford Grammar School, that the plays show no evidence of profound book learning, and that the knowledge of kings and courts evident in the plays is no greater than any intelligent young man could have picked up at second hand. Most anti-Shakespeareans are naïve and betray an obvious snobbery. The author of their favorite plays, they imply, must have had a college diploma framed and hung on his study wall like the one in their dentist's office, and obviously so great a writer must have had a title or some equally significant evidence of exalted social background. They forget that genius has a way of cropping up in unexpected places and that none of the great creative writers of the world got his inspiration in a college or university course.

William Shakespeare was the son of John Shakespeare of Stratford-upon-Avon, a substantial citizen of that small but busy market town in the center of the rich agricultural county of Warwick. John Shakespeare kept a shop, what we would call a general store; he dealt in wool and other produce and gradually acquired property. As a youth, John Shakespeare had learned the trade of glover and leather worker. There is no contemporary evidence that the elder Shakespeare was a butcher, though the anti-Shakespeareans like to talk about the ignorant "butcher's boy of Stratford." Their only evidence is a statement by gossipy John Aubrey, more than a century after William Shakespeare's birth, that young William followed his father's trade, and when he killed a calf, "he would do it in a high style and make a speech." We would like to believe the story true, but Aubrey is not a very credible witness.

John Shakespeare probably continued to operate a farm at Snitterfield that his father had leased. He married Mary Arden, daughter of his father's landlord, a man of some property. The third of their eight children was William, baptized on April 26, 1564, and probably born three days before. At least, it is conventional to celebrate April 23 as his birthday.

The Stratford records give considerable information about John Shakespeare. We know that he held several municipal offices including those of alderman and mayor. In 1580 he was in some sort of legal difficulty and was fined for neglecting a summons of the Court of Queen's Bench requiring him to appear at Westminster and be bound over to keep the peace.

As a citizen and alderman of Stratford, John Shakespeare was entitled to send his son to the grammar school free. Though the records are lost, there can be no reason to doubt that this is where young William received his education. As any student of the period knows, the grammar schools provided the basic education in Latin learning and literature. The Elizabethan grammar school is not to be confused with modern grammar schools. Many cultivated men of the day received all their formal education in the grammar schools. At the universities in this period a student would have received little training that would have inspired him to be a creative writer. At Stratford young Shakespeare would have acquired a familiarity with Latin and some little knowledge of Greek. He would have read Latin authors and become acquainted with the plays of Plautus and Terence. Undoubtedly, in this period of his life he received that stimulation to read and explore for himself the world of ancient and modern history which he later utilized in his plays. The youngster who does not acquire this type of intellectual curiosity *before* college days rarely develops as a result of a college course the kind of mind Shakespeare demonstrated. His learning in books was anything but profound, but he clearly had the probing curiosity that sent him in search of information, and he had a keenness in the observation of nature and of humankind that finds reflection in his poetry.

There is little documentation for Shakespeare's boyhood. There is little reason why there should be. Nobody knew that he was going to be a dramatist about whom any scrap of information would be prized in the centuries to come. He was merely an active and vigorous youth of Stratford, perhaps assisting his father in his business, and no Boswell bothered to write down facts about him. The most important record that we have is a marriage license issued by the Bishop of Worcester on November 27, 1582, to permit William Shakespeare to marry

Anne Hathaway, seven or eight years his senior; furthermore, the Bishop permitted the marriage after reading the banns only once instead of three times, evidence of the desire for haste. The need was explained on May 26, 1583, when the christening of Susanna, daughter of William and Anne Shakespeare, was recorded at Stratford. Two years later, on February 2, 1585, the records show the birth of twins to the Shakespeares, a boy and a girl who were christened Hamnet and Judith.

What William Shakespeare was doing in Stratford during the early years of his married life, or when he went to London, we do not know. It has been conjectured that he tried his hand at schoolteaching, but that is a mere guess. There is a legend that he left Stratford to escape a charge of poaching in the park of Sir Thomas Lucy of Charlecote, but there is no proof of this. There is also a legend that when first he came to London he earned his living by holding horses outside a playhouse and presently was given employment inside, but there is nothing better than eighteenth-century hearsay for this. How Shakespeare broke into the London theatres as a dramatist and actor we do not know. But lack of information is not surprising, for Elizabethans did not write their autobiographies, and we know even less about the lives of many writers and some men of affairs than we know about Shakespeare. By 1592 he was so well established and popular that he incurred the envy of the dramatist and pamphleteer Robert Greene, who referred to him as an "upstart crow . . . in his own conceit the only Shake-scene in a country." From this time onward, contemporary allusions and references in legal documents enable the scholar to chart Shakespeare's career with greater accuracy than is possible with most other Elizabethan dramatists.

By 1594 Shakespeare was a member of the company of actors known as the Lord Chamberlain's Men. After the accession of James I, in 1603, the company would have the sovereign for their patron and would be known as the King's Men. During the period of its greatest prosperity, this company would have as its principal theatres the Globe and the Blackfriars. Shakespeare was both an actor and a shareholder in the company. Tradition has assigned him such acting roles as Adam in *As You Like It* and the Ghost in *Hamlet,* a modest place on the stage that suggests that he may have had other duties in the management of the company. Such conclusions, however, are based on surmise.

What we do know is that his plays were popular and that he was highly successful in his vocation. His first play may have been *The Comedy of Errors,* acted perhaps in 1591. Certainly this was one of his earliest plays. The three parts of *Henry VI* were acted sometime between 1590 and 1592. Critics are not in agreement about precisely how much Shakespeare wrote of these three plays.

Richard III probably dates from 1593. With this play Shakespeare captured the imagination of Elizabethan audiences, then enormously interested in historical plays. With *Richard III* Shakespeare also gave an interpretation pleasing to the Tudors of the rise to power of the grandfather of Queen Elizabeth. From this time onward, Shakespeare's plays followed on the stage in rapid succession: *Titus Andronicus, The Taming of the Shrew, The Two Gentlemen of Verona, Love's Labor's Lost, Romeo and Juliet, Richard II, A Midsummer Night's Dream, King John, The Merchant of Venice, Henry IV (Parts 1 and 2), Much Ado about Nothing, Henry V, Julius Cæsar, As You Like It, Twelfth Night, Hamlet, The Merry Wives of Windsor, All's Well That Ends Well, Measure for Measure, Othello, King Lear,* and nine others that followed before Shakespeare retired completely, about 1613.

In the course of his career in London, he made enough money to enable him to retire to Stratford with a competence. His purchase on May 4, 1597, of New Place, then the second-largest dwelling in Stratford, "a pretty house of brick and timber," with a handsome garden, indicates his increasing prosperity. There his wife and children lived while he busied himself in the London theatres. The summer before he acquired New Place, his life was darkened by the death of his only son, Hamnet, a child of eleven. In May, 1602, Shakespeare purchased one hundred and seven acres of fertile farmland near Stratford and a few months later bought a cottage and garden across the alley from New Place. About 1611, he seems to have returned permanently to Stratford, for the next year a legal document refers to him as "William Shakespeare of Stratford-upon-Avon . . . gentleman." To achieve the desired appellation of gentleman, William Shakespeare had seen to it that the College of Heralds in 1596 granted his father a coat of arms. In one step he thus became a second-generation gentleman.

Shakespeare's daughter Susanna made a good match in 1607 with Dr. John Hall, a prominent and prosperous Stratford physician. His second daughter, Judith, did not marry until she was thirty-one years old, and then, under somewhat scandalous circumstances, she married Thomas Quiney, a Stratford vintner. On March 25, 1616, Shakespeare made his will, bequeathing his landed property to Susanna, £300 to Judith, certain sums to other relatives, and his second-best bed to his wife, Anne. Much has been made of the second-best bed, but the legacy probably indicates only that Anne liked that particular bed. Shakespeare, following the practice of the time, may have already arranged with Susanna for his wife's care. Finally, on April 23, 1616, the anniversary of his birth, William Shakespeare died, and he was buried on April 25 within the chancel of Trinity Church, as befitted an honored citizen. On August 6, 1623, a few months before the publication of the collected edition of Shakespeare's plays, Anne Shakespeare joined her husband in death.

THE PUBLICATION OF HIS PLAYS

During his lifetime Shakespeare made no effort to publish any of his plays, though eighteen appeared in print in single-play editions known as quartos. Some of these are corrupt versions known as "bad quartos." No quarto, so far as is known, had the author's approval. Plays were not considered "literature" any more than most radio and television scripts today are considered literature. Dramatists sold their plays outright to the theatrical companies and it was usually considered in the company's interest to keep plays from getting into print. To achieve a reputation as a man of letters, Shakespeare wrote his *Sonnets* and his narrative poems, *Venus and Adonis* and *The Rape of Lucrece*, but he probably never dreamed that his plays would establish his reputation as a literary genius. Only Ben Jonson, a man known for his colossal conceit, had the crust to call his plays *Works*, as he did when he published an edition in 1616. But men laughed at Ben Jonson.

After Shakespeare's death, two of his old colleagues in the King's Men, John Heminges and Henry Condell, decided that it would be a good thing to print, in more accurate versions than were then available, the plays already published and eighteen additional plays not previously published in quarto. In 1623 appeared *Mr. William Shakespeares Comedies, Histories, & Tragedies. Published according to the True Originall Copies. London. Printed by Isaac Iaggard and Ed. Blount.* This was the famous First Folio, a work that had the authority of Shakespeare's associates. The only play commonly attributed to Shakespeare that was omitted in the First Folio was *Pericles.* In their preface, "To the great Variety of Readers," Heminges and Condell state that whereas "you were abused with diverse stolen and surreptitious copies, maimed and deformed by the frauds and stealths of injurious impostors that exposed them, even those are now offered to your view cured and perfect of their limbs; and all the rest, absolute in their numbers, as he conceived them." What they used for printer's copy is one of the vexed problems of scholarship, and skilled bibliographers have devoted years of study to the question of the relation of the "copy" for the First Folio to Shakespeare's manuscripts. In some cases it is clear that the editors corrected printed quarto versions of the plays, probably by comparison with playhouse scripts. Whether these scripts were in Shakespeare's autograph is anybody's guess. No manuscript of any play in Shakespeare's handwriting has survived. Indeed, very few play manuscripts from this period by any author are extant. The Tudor and Stuart periods had not yet learned to prize autographs and authors' original manuscripts.

Since the First Folio contains eighteen plays not previously printed, it is the only source for these. For the other eighteen, which had appeared in quarto versions, the First Folio also has the authority of an edition prepared and overseen by Shakespeare's colleagues and professional associates. But since editorial standards in 1623 were far from strict, and Heminges and Condell were actors rather than editors by profession, the texts are sometimes careless. The printing and proofreading of the First Folio also left much to be desired, and some garbled passages have had to be corrected and emended. The "good quarto" texts have to be taken into account in preparing a modern edition.

Because of the great popularity of Shakespeare through the centuries, the First Folio has become a prized book, but it is not a very rare one, for it is estimated that 238 copies are extant. The Folger Shakespeare Library in Washington, D.C., has seventy-nine copies of the First Folio, collected by the founder, Henry Clay Folger, who believed that a collation of as many texts as possible would reveal significant facts about the text of Shakespeare's plays. Dr. Charlton Hinman, using an ingenious machine of his own invention for mechanical collating, has made many discoveries that throw light on Shakespeare's text and on printing practices of the day.

The probability is that the First Folio of 1623 had an edition of between 1,000 and 1,250 copies. It is believed that it sold for £1, which made it an expensive book, for £1 in 1623 was equivalent to something between $40 and $50 in modern purchasing power.

During the seventeenth century, Shakespeare was sufficiently popular to warrant three later editions in folio size, the Second Folio of 1632, the Third Folio of 1663–1664, and the Fourth Folio of 1685. The Third Folio added six other plays ascribed to Shakespeare, but these are apocryphal.

THE SHAKESPEAREAN THEATRE

The theatres in which Shakespeare's plays were performed were vastly different from those we know today. The stage was a platform that jutted out into the area now occupied by the first rows of seats on the main floor, what is called the "orchestra" in America and the "pit" in England. This platform had no curtain to come down at the ends of acts and scenes. And although simple stage properties were available, the Elizabethan theatre lacked both the machinery and the elaborate movable scenery of the modern theatre. In the rear of the platform stage was a curtained area that could be used as an inner room, a tomb, or any such scene that might be required. A balcony above this inner room, and perhaps balconies on the sides of the stage, could represent the upper deck of a ship, the entry to Juliet's room, or a prison window. A trap door in the stage provided an entrance for ghosts and devils from the nether regions, and a similar trap in the canopied structure over the stage, known as the "heavens," made it possible to let down angels on a rope. These primitive stage arrangements help to account for many elements in Elizabethan plays. For example, since there was no curtain, the dramatist frequently felt the necessity of writing into his play action to clear the stage at the ends of acts and scenes. The funeral march at the end of *Hamlet* is not there merely for atmosphere; Shakespeare had to get the corpses off the stage. The lack of scenery also freed the dramatist from undue concern about the exact location of his sets, and the physical relation of his various settings to each other did not have to be worked out with the same precision as in the modern theatre.

Before London had buildings designed exclusively for theatrical entertainment, plays were given in inns and taverns. The characteristic inn of the period had an inner courtyard with rooms opening onto balconies overlooking the yard. Players could set up their temporary stages at one end of the yard and audiences could find seats on the balconies out of the weather. The poorer sort could stand or sit on the cobblestones in the yard, which was open to the sky. The first theatres followed this construction, and throughout the Elizabethan period the large public theatres had a yard in front of the stage open to the weather, with two or three tiers of covered balconies extending around the theatre. This physical structure again influenced the writing of plays. Because a dramatist wanted the actors to be heard, he frequently wrote into his play orations that could be delivered with declamatory effect. He also provided spectacle, buffoonery, and broad jests to keep the riotous groundlings in the yard entertained and quiet.

In another respect the Elizabethan theatre differed greatly from ours. It had no actresses. All women's roles were taken by boys, sometimes recruited from the boys' choirs of the London churches. Some of these youths acted their roles with great skill and the Elizabethans did not seem to be aware of any incongruity. The first actresses on the professional English stage appeared after the Restoration of Charles II, in 1660, when exiled Englishmen brought back from France practices of the French stage.

London in the Elizabethan period, as now, was the center of theatrical interest, though wandering actors from time to time traveled through the country performing in inns, halls, and the houses of the nobility. The first professional playhouse, called simply The Theatre, was erected by James Burbage, father of Shakespeare's colleague Richard Burbage, in 1576 on lands of the old Holywell

Priory adjacent to Finsbury Fields, a playground and park area just north of the city walls. It had the advantage of being outside the city's jurisdiction and yet was near enough to be easily accessible. Soon after The Theatre was opened, another playhouse called The Curtain was erected in the same neighborhood. Both of these playhouses had open courtyards and were probably polygonal in shape.

About the time The Curtain opened, Richard Farrant, Master of the Children of the Chapel Royal at Windsor and of St. Paul's, conceived the idea of opening a "private" theatre in the old monastery buildings of the Blackfriars, not far from St. Paul's Cathedral in the heart of the city. This theatre was ostensibly to train the choirboys in plays for presentation at Court, but Farrant managed to present plays to paying audiences and achieved considerable success until aristocratic neighbors complained and had the theatre closed. The first Blackfriars Theatre was significant, however, because it popularized the boy actors in a professional way and it paved the way for a second theatre in the Blackfriars, which Shakespeare's company took over more than thirty years later. By the last years of the sixteenth century, London had at least six professional theatres and still others were erected during the reign of James I.

The Globe Theatre, the playhouse that most people connect with Shakespeare, was erected early in 1599 on the Bankside, the area across the Thames from the city. Its construction had a dramatic beginning, for on the night of December 28, 1598, James Burbage's sons, Cuthbert and Richard, gathered together a crew who tore down the old theatre in Holywell and carted the timbers across the river to a site that they had chosen for a new playhouse. The reason for this clandestine operation was a row with the landowner over the lease to the Holywell property. The site chosen for the Globe was another playground outside of the city's jurisdiction, a region of somewhat unsavory character. Not far away was the Bear Garden, an amphitheatre devoted to the baiting of bears and bulls. This was also the region occupied by many houses of ill fame licensed by the Bishop of Winchester and the source of substantial revenue to him. But it was easily accessible either from London Bridge or by means of the cheap boats operated by the London watermen, and it had the great advantage of being beyond the authority of the Puritanical aldermen of London, who frowned on plays because they lured apprentices from work, filled their heads with improper ideas, and generally exerted a bad influence. The aldermen also complained that the crowds drawn together in the theatre helped to spread the plague.

The Globe was the handsomest theatre up to its time. It was a large building, apparently octagonal in shape, and open like its predecessors to the sky in the center, but capable of seating a large audience in its covered balconies. To erect and operate the Globe, the Burbages organized a syndicate composed of the leading members of the dramatic company, of which Shakespeare was a member. Since it was open to the weather and depended on natural light, plays had to be given in the afternoon. This caused no hardship in the long afternoons of an English summer, but in the winter the weather was a great handicap and discouraged all except the hardiest. For that reason, in 1608 Shakespeare's company was glad to take over the lease of the second Blackfriars Theatre, a substantial, roomy hall reconstructed within the framework of the old monastery building. This theatre was protected from the weather and its stage was artificially lighted by chandeliers of candles. This became the winter playhouse for Shakespeare's company and at once proved so popular that the congestion of traffic created an embarrassing problem. Stringent regulations had to be made for the movement of coaches in the vicinity. Shakespeare's company continued to use the Globe during the summer months. In 1613 a squib fired from a cannon during a performance of *Henry VIII* fell on the thatched roof and the Globe burned to the ground. The next year it was rebuilt.

London had other famous theatres. The Rose, just west of the Globe, was built by Philip Henslowe, a semiliterate denizen of the Bankside, who became one of the most important theatrical owners and producers of the Tudor and Stuart periods. What is more important for historians, he kept a detailed account book, which provides much of our information about theatrical history in his time. Another famous theatre on the Bankside was the Swan, which a Dutch priest, Johannes de Witt, visited in 1596. The crude drawing of the stage which he made was copied by his friend Arend van Buchell; it is one of the important pieces of contemporary evidence for theatrical construction. Among the other theatres, the Fortune, north of the city, on Golding Lane, and the Red Bull, even farther away from the city, off St. John's Street, were the most popular. The Red Bull, much frequented by apprentices, favored sensational and sometimes rowdy plays.

The actors who kept all of these theatres going were organized into companies under the protection of some noble patron. Traditionally actors had enjoyed a low reputation. In some of the ordinances they were classed as vagrants; in the phraseology of the time, "rogues, vagabonds, sturdy beggars, and common players" were all listed together as undesirables. To escape penalties often meted out to these characters, organized groups of actors managed to gain the protection of various personages of high degree. In the later years of Elizabeth's reign, a group flourished under the name of the Queen's Men; another group had the protection of the Lord Admiral and were known as the Lord Admiral's Men. Edward Alleyn, son-in-law of Philip

Henslowe, was the leading spirit in the Lord Admiral's Men. Besides the adult companies, troupes of boy actors from time to time also enjoyed considerable popularity. Among these were the Children of Paul's and the Children of the Chapel Royal.

The company with which Shakespeare had a long association had for its first patron Henry Carey, Lord Hunsdon, the Lord Chamberlain, and hence they were known as the Lord Chamberlain's Men. After the accession of James I, they became the King's Men. This company was the great rival of the Lord Admiral's Men, managed by Henslowe and Alleyn.

All was not easy for the players in Shakespeare's time, for the aldermen of London were always eager for an excuse to close up the Blackfriars and any other theatres in their jurisdiction. The theatres outside the jurisdiction of London were not immune from interference, for they might be shut up by order of the Privy Council for meddling in politics or for various other offenses, or they might be closed in time of plague lest they spread infection. During plague times, the actors usually went on tour and played the provinces wherever they could find an audience. Particularly frightening were the plagues of 1592–1594 and 1613 when the theatres closed and the players, like many other Londoners, had to take to the country.

Though players had a low social status, they enjoyed great popularity, and one of the favorite forms of entertainment at Court was the performance of plays. To be commanded to perform at Court conferred great prestige upon a company of players, and printers frequently noted that fact when they published plays. Several of Shakespeare's plays were performed before the sovereign, and Shakespeare himself undoubtedly acted in some of these plays.

REFERENCES FOR FURTHER READING

Many readers will want suggestions for further reading about Shakespeare and his times. A few references will serve as guides to further study in the enormous literature on the subject. A simple and useful little book is Gerald Sanders, *A Shakespeare Primer* (New York, 1950). *A Companion to Shakespeare Studies,* edited by Harley Granville-Barker and G. B. Harrison (Cambridge, 1934), is a valuable guide. The most recent concise handbook of facts about Shakespeare is Gerald E. Bentley, *Shakespeare: A Biographical Handbook* (New Haven, 1961). More detailed but not so voluminous as to be confusing is Hazelton Spencer, *The Art and Life of William Shakespeare* (New York, 1940), which, like Sanders' and Bentley's handbooks, contains a brief annotated list of useful books on various aspects of the subject. The most detailed and scholarly work providing complete factual information about Shakespeare is Sir Edmund Chambers, *William Shakespeare: A Study of Facts and Problems* (2 vols., Oxford, 1930).

Among other biographies of Shakespeare, Joseph Quincy Adams, *A Life of William Shakespeare* (Boston, 1923) is still an excellent assessment of the essential facts and the traditional information, and Marchette Chute, *Shakespeare of London* (New York, 1949; paperback, 1957) stresses Shakespeare's life in the theatre. Two new biographies of Shakespeare have recently appeared. A. L. Rowse, *William Shakespeare: A Biography* (London, 1963; New York, 1964) provides an appraisal by a distinguished English historian, who dismisses the notion that somebody else wrote Shakespeare's plays as arrant nonsense that runs counter to known historical fact. Peter Quennell, *Shakespeare: A Biography* (Cleveland and New York, 1963) is a sensitive and intelligent survey of what is known and surmised of Shakespeare's life. Louis B. Wright, *Shakespeare for Everyman* (New York, 1964; 1965) discusses the basis of Shakespeare's enduring popularity.

The *Shakespeare Quarterly*, published by the Shakespeare Association of America under the editorship of James G. McManaway, is recommended for those who wish to keep up with current Shakespearean scholarship and stage productions. The *Quarterly* includes an annual bibliography of Shakespeare editions and works on Shakespeare published during the previous year.

The question of the authenticity of Shakespeare's plays arouses perennial attention. The theory of hidden cryptograms in the plays is demolished by William F. and Elizebeth S. Friedman, *The Shakespearean Ciphers Examined* (New York, 1957). A succinct account of the various absurdities advanced to suggest the authorship of a multitude of candidates other than Shakespeare will be found in R. C. Churchill, *Shakespeare and His Betters* (Bloomington, Ind., 1959). Another recent discussion of the subject, *The Authorship of Shakespeare*, by James G. McManaway (Washington, D.C., 1962), presents the evidence from contemporary records to prove the identity of Shakespeare the actor-playwright with Shakespeare of Stratford.

Scholars are not in agreement about the details of playhouse construction in the Elizabethan period. John C. Adams presents a plausible reconstruction of the Globe in *The Globe Playhouse: Its Design and Equipment* (Cambridge, Mass., 1942; 2nd rev. ed., 1961). A description with excellent drawings based on Dr. Adams' model is Irwin Smith, *Shakespeare's Globe Playhouse: A Modern Reconstruction in Text and Scale Drawings* (New York, 1956). Other sensible discussions are W. Walter Hodges, *The Globe Restored* (London, 1953) and A. M. Nagler, *Shakespeare's Stage* (New Haven, 1958). Bernard Beckerman, *Shakespeare at the Globe, 1599–1609* (New Haven, 1962; paperback, 1962) discusses Elizabethan staging and acting techniques.

A sound and readable history of the early theatres is Joseph Quincy Adams, *Shakespearean Playhouses: A History of English Theatres from the Beginnings to the Restoration* (Boston, 1917). For detailed, factual information about the Elizabethan and seventeenth-century stages, the definitive reference works are Sir Edmund Chambers, *The Elizabethan Stage* (4 vols., Oxford, 1923) and Gerald E. Bentley, *The Jacobean and Caroline Stages* (5 vols., Oxford, 1941–1956).

Further information on the history of the theatre and related topics will be found in the following titles: T. W. Baldwin, *The Organization and Personnel of the Shakespearean Company* (Princeton, 1927); Lily Bess Campbell, *Scenes and Machines on the English Stage during the Renaissance* (Cambridge, 1923); Esther Cloudman Dunn, *Shakespeare in America* (New York, 1939); George C. D. Odell, *Shakespeare from Betterton to Irving* (2 vols., London, 1931); Arthur Colby Sprague, *Shakespeare and the Actors: The Stage Business in His Plays (1660–1905)* (Cambridge, Mass., 1944) and *Shakepecrian Players and Performances* (Cambridge, Mass., 1953); Leslie Hotson, *The Commonwealth and Restoration Stage* (Cambridge, Mass., 1928); Alwin Thaler, *Shakspere to Sheridan: A Book about the Theatre of Yesterday and To-day* (Cambridge, Mass., 1922); George C. Branam, *Eighteenth-Century Adaptations of Shakespeare's Tragedies* (Berkeley, 1956); C. Beecher Hogan, *Shakespeare in the*

Theatre, 1701–1800 (Oxford, 1957); Ernest Bradlee Watson, *Sheridan to Robertson: A Study of the 19th-Century London Stage* (Cambridge, Mass., 1926); and Enid Welsford, *The Court Masque* (Cambridge, Mass., 1927).

A brief account of the growth of Shakespeare's reputation is F. E. Halliday, *The Cult of Shakespeare* (London, 1947). A more detailed discussion is given in Augustus Ralli, *A History of Shakespearian Criticism* (2 vols., Oxford, 1932; New York, 1958). Harley Granville-Barker, *Prefaces to Shakespeare* (5 vols., London, 1927–1948; 2 vols., London, 1958) provides stimulating critical discussion of the plays. An older classic of criticism is Andrew C. Bradley, *Shakespearean Tragedy: Lectures on Hamlet, Othello, King Lear, Macbeth* (London, 1904; paperback, 1955). Sir Edmund Chambers, *Shakespeare: A Survey* (London, 1935; paperback, 1958) contains short, sensible essays on thirty-four of the plays, originally written as introductions to single-play editions. Alfred Harbage, *William Shakespeare: A Reader's Guide* (New York, 1963) is a handbook to the reading and appreciation of the plays, with scene synopses and interpretation.

For the history plays see Lily Bess Campbell, *Shakespeare's "Histories": Mirrors of Elizabethan Policy* (Cambridge, 1947); John Palmer, *Political Characters of Shakespeare* (London, 1945; 1961); E. M. W. Tillyard, *Shakespeare's History Plays* (London, 1948); Irving Ribner, *The English History*

Play in the Age of Shakespeare (Princeton, 1947; rev. ed., New York, 1965); Max M. Reese, *The Cease of Majesty* (London, 1961); and Arthur Colby Sprague, *Shakespeare's Histories: Plays for the Stage* (London, 1964). Harold Jenkins, "Shakespeare's History Plays: 1900–1951," *Shakespeare Survey 6* (Cambridge, 1953), 1–15, provides an excellent survey of recent critical opinion on the subject.

Of particular value for the study of the problems of *Titus Andronicus* is Geoffrey Bullough, *Narrative and Dramatic Sources of Shakespeare*, Vol. VI (London, 1966), which reprints the Folger Library copy of the anonymous eighteenth-century prose narrative, *The History of Titus Andronicus*. Professor Bullough thinks it possible that this may derive from a sixteenth-century original, which Shakespeare could have used as a source. As to the authorship, he concludes that "Shakespeare planned the play and probably wrote most of it" (p. 32). Professor Hereward T. Price argues for Shakespeare's responsibility for the play in "The Authorship of *Titus Andronicus*," *Journal of English and Germanic Philology*, XLII (1943), 55–81.

The introduction to J. Q. Adams' facsimile edition of *Shakespeare's Titus Andronicus: The First Quarto, 1594* (New York, 1936) discusses date, source, and early printings of the play. Professor Adams was the first to call attention to the Folger's prose narrative and to suggest that it might derive from Shakespeare's main source. Another useful study of the problems of authorship is Austin K. Gray, "Shakespeare and *Titus Andronicus*," *Studies in Philology*, XXV (1928), 295–311. A stylistic study of the play is provided by R. F. Hill, "The Composition of *Titus Andronicus*," *Shakespeare Survey 10* (Cambridge, 1957), 60–70. The same volume contains an illuminating discussion of Shakespeare's use of Roman material in T. J. B. Spencer's "Shakespeare and the Elizabethan Romans," and an analysis of the Ovidian and Senecan influences on the play in Eugene M. Waith's "The Metamorphosis of Violence in *Titus Andronicus*."

The comedies are illuminated by the following studies: C. L. Barber, *Shakespeare's Festive Comedy* (Princeton, 1959); John Russell Brown, *Shakespeare and His Comedies* (London, 1957); H. B. Charlton, *Shakespearian Comedy* (London, 1938; 4th ed., 1949); W. W. Lawrence, *Shakespeare's Problem Comedies* (New York, 1931); and Thomas M. Parrott, *Shakespearean Comedy* (New York, 1949).

Further discussions of Shakespeare's tragedies, in addition to Bradley, already cited, are contained in H. B. Charlton, *Shakespearian Tragedy* (Cambridge, 1948); Willard Farnham, *The Medieval Heritage of Elizabethan Tragedy* (Berkeley, 1936) and *Shakespeare's Tragic Frontier: The World of His Final Tragedies* (Berkeley, 1950); and Harold S. Wilson, *On the Design of Shakespearian Tragedy* (Toronto, 1957).

Kenneth Muir, *Shakespeare's Sources: Comedies*

and Tragedies (London, 1957) discusses Shakespeare's use of source material. The sources themselves have been reprinted several times. Among old editions are John P. Collier (ed.), *Shakespeare's Library* (2 vols., London, 1850), Israel C. Gollancz (ed.), *The Shakespeare Classics* (12 vols., London, 1907–1926), and W. C. Hazlitt (ed.), *Shakespeare's Library* (6 vols., London, 1875). A modern edition is being prepared by Geoffrey Bullough with the title *Narrative and Dramatic Sources of Shakespeare* (London and New York, 1957–). Six volumes, covering the sources for all the plays except the tragedies, have been published to date (1967).

In addition to the second edition of *Webster's New International Dictionary,* which contains most of the unusual words used by Shakespeare, the following reference works are helpful: Edwin A. Abbott, *A Shakespearian Grammar* (London, 1872; reprinted in paperback, 1966); C. T. Onions, *A Shakespeare Glossary* (2nd rev. ed., Oxford, 1925); and Eric Partridge, *Shakespeare's Bawdy* (New York, 1948; paperback, 1960).

Some knowledge of the social background of the period in which Shakespeare lived is important for a full understanding of his work. A brief, clear, and accurate account of Tudor history is S. T. Bindoff, *The Tudors,* in the Penguin series. A readable general history is G. M. Trevelyan, *The History of England,* first published in 1926 and available in numerous editions. The same author's *English Social His-*

tory, first published in 1942 and also available in many editions, provides fascinating information about England in all periods. Sir John Neale, *Queen Elizabeth* (London, 1935; paperback, 1957) is the best study of the great Queen. Various aspects of life in the Elizabethan period are treated in Louis B. Wright, *Middle-class Culture in Elizabethan England* (Chapel Hill, N.C., 1935; reprinted Ithaca, N.Y., 1958, 1964). *Shakespeare's England: An Account of the Life and Manners of His Age*, edited by Sidney Lee and C. T. Onions (2 vols., Oxford, 1917), provides much information on many aspects of Elizabethan life. A fascinating survey of the period will be found in Muriel St. C. Byrne, *Elizabethan Life in Town and Country* (London, 1925; rev. ed., 1954; paperback, 1961).

The Folger Library is issuing a series of illustrated booklets entitled "Folger Booklets on Tudor and Stuart Civilization," printed and distributed by Cornell University Press. Published to date are the following titles:

D. W. Davies, *Dutch Influences on English Culture, 1558–1625*

Giles E. Dawson, *The Life of William Shakespeare*

Ellen C. Eyler, *Early English Gardens and Garden Books*

Elaine W. Fowler, *English Sea Power in the Early Tudor Period, 1485–1558*

John R. Hale, *The Art of War and Renaissance England*

William Haller, *Elizabeth I and the Puritans*

Virginia A. LaMar, *English Dress in the Age of Shakespeare*

———, *Travel and Roads in England*

John L. Lievsay, *The Elizabethan Image of Italy*

James G. McManaway, *The Authorship of Shakespeare*

Dorothy E. Mason, *Music in Elizabethan England*

Garrett Mattingly, *The "Invincible" Armada and Elizabethan England*

Boies Penrose, *Tudor and Early Stuart Voyaging*

T. I. Rae, *Scotland in the Time of Shakespeare*

Conyers Read, *The Government of England under Elizabeth*

Albert J. Schmidt, *The Yeoman in Tudor and Stuart England*

Lilly C. Stone, *English Sports and Recreations*

Craig R. Thompson, *The Bible in English, 1525–1611*

———, *The English Church in the Sixteenth Century*

———, *Schools in Tudor England*

———, *Universities in Tudor England*

Louis B. Wright, *Shakespeare's Theatre and the Dramatic Tradition*

At intervals the Folger Library plans to gather these booklets in hardbound volumes. The first is

Life and Letters in Tudor and Stuart England, First Folger Series, edited by Louis B. Wright and Virginia A. LaMar (published for the Folger Shakespeare Library by Cornell University Press, 1962). The volume contains eleven of the separate booklets.

[Dramatis Personae

Saturninus, son of the late Emperor of Rome, afterward Emperor.
Bassianus, brother of *Saturninus*.
Titus Andronicus, a noble Roman general.
Marcus Andronicus, tribune of the people and brother of *Titus*.

Lucius,
Quintus, } sons of *Titus Andronicus*.
Martius,
Mutius,

Young Lucius, son of *Lucius Andronicus*.
Publius, son of *Marcus Andronicus*.

Sempronius,
Caius, } kinsmen of *Titus*.
Valentine,

Aemilius, a noble Roman.

Alarbus,
Demetrius, } sons of *Tamora*.
Chiron,

Aaron, a Moor, beloved of *Tamora*.
A Captain, a Tribune, a Messenger, and a Clown; Romans and Goths.

Tamora, Queen of the Goths.
Lavinia, daughter of *Titus Andronicus*.
A Nurse.
Senators, Tribunes, Officers, Soldiers, and Attendants.

SCENE: *Rome and the country near it.*]

xlv

Dramatis Personæ

TITUS
ANDRONICUS

ACT I

I. i. Saturninus and Bassianus, sons of the deceased Roman Emperor, both claim the succession, but Titus Andronicus is the people's choice. Titus appears in triumph with Tamora, the Queen of the Goths, and her sons as captives and persuades the people to accept Saturninus. Titus brings with him for burial the bodies of two sons slain in battle and selects Alarbus, eldest son of Tamora, to be sacrificed to appease their spirits. Tamora's appeal to spare Alarbus' life is denied, and the sacrifice is performed. In gratitude for Titus' support, Saturninus promises to marry Titus' daughter, Lavinia, but Bassianus seizes Lavinia, who had been betrothed to him, and carries her off. Titus' sons assist Bassianus, and Titus kills Mutius for preventing his pursuit. Resentful, Saturninus forgets his debt to Titus and determines to marry Tamora. After the marriage rites, Saturninus threatens to make Bassianus and the Andronici suffer for the abduction of Lavinia, but Tamora pretends to make peace, assuring her husband privately that she will find a way to destroy all the Andronici. Saturninus outwardly shows forgiveness and agrees to join a hunt that Titus proposes for the next morning.

―――――――――――――

4. **successive:** inherited.

5. **his first-born son that:** the first-born son of him who.

6. **ware:** wore.

8. **mine age:** i.e., his rights as the oldest son.

(Continued on next page)

ACT I

Scene I. [Rome. Before the Senate House, the Tomb
of the Andronici appearing.]

*Enter the Tribunes and Senators aloft. And then enter
Saturninus and his Followers at one door, and Bassianus and his Followers with Drums and Trumpets at
the other.*

   Sat. Noble patricians, patrons of my right,
Defend the justice of my cause with arms;
And, countrymen, my loving followers,
Plead my successive title with your swords.
I am his first-born son that was the last   5
That ware the imperial diadem of Rome:
Then let my father's honors live in me,
Nor wrong mine age with this indignity.
   Bass. Romans, friends, followers, favorers of my
      right,   10
If ever Bassianus, Caesar's son,
Were gracious in the eyes of royal Rome,
Keep then this passage to the Capitol;
And suffer not dishonor to approach
The imperial seat, to virtue consecrate,   15

11. **Caesar's son:** the son of the previous Emperor. The characters of the play are not historical, although some of the incidents are taken from Rome's long history. Gothic invasions occurred in the fifth century A.D.

12. **gracious:** pleasing.

15. **to virtue consecrate:** consecrated to virtue.

* * *

16. **continence:** discipline.

17. **let desert in pure election shine:** i.e., single out the person whose sheer merit warrants his election.

20. **rule and empery:** imperial rule.

21. **people:** i.e., the plebeians.

23. **empery:** empire.

25. **good and great deserts to Rome:** great benefactions performed for Rome.

28. **accited:** summoned.

31. **yoked:** conquered.

36. **field:** the First Quarto only has three and a half additional lines here: "field, and at this day,/ To the Monument of that Andronicy/ Done sacrifice of expiation,/ And slaine the Noblest prisoner of the Gothes." Presumably Shakespeare later decided to dramatize the sacrifice to Alarbus to give Tamora's revenge stronger motivation.

40. **his name:** i.e., whichever man.

To justice, continence, and nobility:
But let desert in pure election shine;
And, Romans, fight for freedom in your choice.

Enter Marcus Andronicus, aloft, with the crown.

Mar. Princes, that strive by factions and by friends
Ambitiously for rule and empery, 20
Know that the people of Rome, for whom we stand
A special party, have by common voice,
In election for the Roman empery,
Chosen Andronicus, surnamed Pius
For many good and great deserts to Rome. 25
A nobler man, a braver warrior,
Lives not this day within the city walls.
He by the Senate is accited home
From weary wars against the barbarous Goths,
That, with his sons, a terror to our foes, 30
Hath yoked a nation strong, trained up in arms.
Ten years are spent since first he undertook
This cause of Rome and chastised with arms
Our enemies' pride. Five times he hath returned
Bleeding to Rome, bearing his valiant sons 35
In coffins from the field.
And now at last, laden with honor's spoils,
Returns the good Andronicus to Rome,
Renowned Titus, flourishing in arms.
Let us entreat, by honor of his name 40
Whom worthily you would have now succeed,
And in the Capitol and Senate's right,

44. **abate:** decrease.
47. **fair:** moderately.
49. **affy:** trust.
64. **confident and kind:** loyally trusting.
SD 66. **Flourish:** a series of trumpet.

The Capitol. From Giovanni Bartolommeo Marliani, *Urbis Romae topographia* (1588).

Whom you pretend to honor and adore,
That you withdraw you and abate your strength,
Dismiss your followers and, as suitors should,   45
Plead your deserts in peace and humbleness.

  Sat. How fair the Tribune speaks to calm my
    thoughts!

  Bass. Marcus Andronicus, so I do affy
In thy uprightness and integrity,   50
And so I love and honor thee and thine,
Thy noble brother Titus and his sons,
And her to whom my thoughts are humbled all,
Gracious Lavinia, Rome's rich ornament,
That I will here dismiss my loving friends   55
And to my fortunes and the people's favor
Commit my cause in balance to be weighed.
                 Exeunt Soldiers of Bassianus.

  Sat. Friends, that have been thus forward in my
    right,
I thank you all and here dismiss you all,   60
And to the love and favor of my country
Commit myself, my person and the cause.
                 Exeunt Soldiers of Saturninus.
Rome, be as just and gracious unto me
As I am confident and kind to thee.
Open the gates and let me in.   65

  Bass. Tribunes, and me, a poor competitor.

Flourish. [*Saturninus and Bassianus*] *go up into the*
                         Senate House.

70. **With honor and with fortune:** with honorable fortune.

71. **circumscribed:** surrounded.

74. **weeds:** garments.

75. **Lo:** just; **his:** its; **fraught:** freight.

82. **gracious:** favorable.

A Roman soldier. From Guillaume du Choul, *Discours de la religion des anciens Romains* (1581).

Enter a Captain.

Cap. Romans, make way. The good Andronicus,
Patron of virtue, Rome's best champion,
Successful in the battles that he fights,
With honor and with fortune is returned   70
From where he circumscribed with his sword
And brought to yoke the enemies of Rome.

*Sound drums and trumpets; and then enter two sons
of Titus, [Martius and Mutius]; and then two Men
bearing a coffin covered with black; then two other
Sons [Lucius and Quintus]; then Titus Andronicus;
and then Tamora the Queen of Goths with [her son
Alarbus and] her two sons Chiron and Demetrius,
with Aaron the Moor, and others as many as can be.
They set down the coffin, and Titus speaks.*

Titus. Hail, Rome, victorious in thy mourning
    weeds!
Lo, as the bark that hath discharged his fraught   75
Returns with precious lading to the bay
From whence at first she weighed her anchorage,
Cometh Andronicus, bound with laurel boughs,
To re-salute his country with his tears,
Tears of true joy for his return to Rome.   80
Thou great defender of this Capitol,
Stand gracious to the rites that we intend!
Romans, of five-and-twenty valiant sons,
Half of the number that King Priam had,

87. **latest:** last.

90. **unkind:** unnatural.

91. **sufferst:** allowest.

92. **Styx:** the river in Hades, which dead souls could not cross to reach their assigned places until their bodies had been buried.

98. **in store:** stored up.

102. **Ad manes fratrum:** to our brothers' spirits.

104. **shadows:** shades; spirits.

105. **prodigies:** disasters.

110. **passion:** passionate sorrow.

113. **Sufficeth not:** does it not suffice.

Behold the poor remains, alive and dead!   85
These that survive let Rome reward with love;
These that I bring unto their latest home
With burial amongst their ancestors.
Here Goths have given me leave to sheathe my sword.
Titus, unkind, and careless of thine own,   90
Why sufferst thou thy sons, unburied yet,
To hover on the dreadful shore of Styx?
Make way to lay them by their brethren.
                              They open the tomb.
There greet in silence, as the dead are wont,
And sleep in peace, slain in your country's wars!   95
O sacred receptacle of my joys,
Sweet cell of virtue and nobility,
How many sons hast thou of mine in store
That thou wilt never render to me more!
    Luc. Give us the proudest prisoner of the Goths,   100
That we may hew his limbs and on a pile
Ad manes fratrum sacrifice his flesh
Before this earthy prison of their bones,
That so the shadows be not unappeased,
Nor we disturbed with prodigies on earth.   105
    Titus. I give him you, the noblest that survives,
The eldest son of this distressed queen.
    Tam. Stay, Roman brethren! Gracious conqueror,
Victorious Titus, rue the tears I shed,
A mother's tears in passion for her son: 110
And if thy sons were ever dear to thee,
Oh, think my son to be as dear to me!
Sufficeth not that we are brought to Rome
To beautify thy triumphs and return

121. **the nature of the gods:** a proverbial idea: "It is in their mercy that kings come closest to the gods."

123. **badge:** symbol.

125. **Patient:** calm.

131. **straight:** immediately.

134. **irreligious piety:** unholy devotion to family obligation.

136. **Oppose:** compare.

140. **the Queen of Troy:** Hecuba, wife of King Priam.

142. **Thracian tyrant:** King Polymnestor of Thrace, who murdered Hecuba's son, Polydorus; in revenge she had his children killed and plucked out his eyes herself.

Hecuba attacking Polymnestor. From Gabriele Simeoni, *La vita et Metamorfoseo d'Ovidio* (1559).

Captive to thee and to thy Roman yoke, 115
But must my sons be slaughtered in the streets
For valiant doings in their country's cause?
Oh, if to fight for king and commonweal
Were piety in thine, it is in these.
Andronicus, stain not thy tomb with blood. 120
Wilt thou draw near the nature of the gods?
Draw near them then in being merciful.
Sweet mercy is nobility's true badge.
Thrice-noble Titus, spare my first-born son.
  Titus. Patient yourself, madam, and pardon me. 125
These are their brethren, whom your Goths beheld
Alive and dead: and for their brethren slain
Religiously they ask a sacrifice.
To this your son is marked, and die he must
T' appease their groaning shadows that are gone. 130
  Luc. Away with him! and make a fire straight;
And with our swords, upon a pile of wood,
Let's hew his limbs till they be clean consumed.
                    Exeunt Titus' sons with Alarbus.
  Tam. Oh, cruel, irreligious piety!
  Chir. Was never Scythia half so barbarous. 135
  Dem. Oppose not Scythia to ambitious Rome.
Alarbus goes to rest, and we survive
To tremble under Titus' threat'ning look.
Then, madam, stand resolved; but hope withal
The selfsame gods that armed the Queen of Troy 140
With opportunity of sharp revenge
Upon the Thracian tyrant in his tent
May favour Tamora, the Queen of Goths,
When Goths were Goths and Tamora was queen,

145. **quit:** requite; revenge.
151. **larums:** soundings of trumpets.

PATRITIO ANTICO ROM.

A Roman aristocrat. From Cesare Vecellio, *Habiti antichi et moderni di tutto il mondo* (1590).

7

To quit the bloody wrongs upon her foes.   145

*Enter the sons of Andronicus again, [with their
swords bloody].*

  Luc. See, lord and father, how we have performed
Our Roman rites! Alarbus' limbs are lopped
And entrails feed the sacrificing fire,
Whose smoke like incense doth perfume the sky.
Remaineth nought but to inter our brethren   150
And with loud larums welcome them to Rome.
  Titus. Let it be so, and let Andronicus
Make this his latest farewell to their souls.
          Sound trumpets, and lay the coffin in the tomb.
In peace and honor rest you here, my sons;
Rome's readiest champions, repose you here in rest,   155
Secure from worldly chances and mishaps!
Here lurks no treason, here no envy swells,
Here grow no damned drugs, here are no storms,
No noise, but silence and eternal sleep.
In peace and honor rest you here, my sons!   160

Enter Lavinia.

  Lav. In peace and honor live Lord Titus long!
My noble lord and father, live in fame!
Lo, at this tomb my tributary tears
I render for my brethren's obsequies;
And at thy feet I kneel, with tears of joy   165
Shed on this earth, for thy return to Rome.
O bless me here with thy victorious hand,

170. **cordial:** comfort.

172. **date:** duration.

182. **aspired:** attained; **Solon's happiness:** referring to Solon's words to Croesus that no man should call himself happy until he dies (Herodotus). The anecdote became a proverbial caution against complacent enjoyment of good fortune.

186. **their Tribune and their trust:** their trusted Tribune.

187. **palliament:** robe of candidacy.

192. **fits:** befits.

194. **What:** why.

Whose fortunes Rome's best citizens applaud!
  Titus. Kind Rome, that hast thus lovingly reserved
The cordial of mine age to glad my heart!   170
Lavinia, live; outlive thy father's days
And fame's eternal date, for virtue's praise!

[*Enter above Marcus Andronicus and Tribunes; and
        Saturninus and Bassianus, attended.*]

  Mar. Long live Lord Titus, my beloved brother,
Gracious triumpher in the eyes of Rome!
  Titus. Thanks, gentle Tribune, noble brother 175
    Marcus.
  Mar. And welcome, nephews, from successful wars,
You that survive, and you that sleep in fame!
Fair lords, your fortunes are alike in all
That in your country's service drew your swords: 180
But safer triumph is this funeral pomp
That hath aspired to Solon's happiness
And triumphs over chance in honor's bed.
Titus Andronicus, the people of Rome,
Whose friend in justice thou hast ever been,   185
Send thee by me, their Tribune and their trust,
This palliament of white and spotless hue
And name thee in election for the empire
With these our late-deceased Emperor's sons:
Be *Candidatus*, then, and put it on,   190
And help to set a head on headless Rome.
  Titus. A better head her glorious body fits
Than his that shakes for age and feebleness.
What should I don this robe and trouble you?

202. **right and service:** honorable service.

206. **obtain and ask:** cf. the proverb "Ask and have."

207. **canst thou tell:** i.e., "you don't say," an expression of disagreement.

222. **honorable meed:** i.e., virtue is its own reward.

Roman officials and troops. From Guillaume du Choul, *Discours de la religion des anciens Romains* (1581).

Be chosen with proclamations today, 195
Tomorrow yield up rule, resign my life,
And set abroad new business for you all?
Rome, I have been thy soldier forty years,
And led my country's strength successfully,
And buried one-and-twenty valiant sons, 200
Knighted in field, slain manfully in arms,
In right and service of their noble country.
Give me a staff of honor for mine age,
But not a scepter to control the world.
Upright he held it, lords, that held it last. 205
   Mar. Titus, thou shalt obtain and ask the empery.
   Sat. Proud and ambitious Tribune, canst thou tell?
   Titus. Patience, Prince Saturninus.
   Sat.   Romans, do me right!
Patricians, draw your swords, and sheathe them not 210
Till Saturninus be Rome's Emperor.
Andronicus, would thou wert shipped to hell
Rather than rob me of the people's hearts!
   Luc. Proud Saturnine, interrupter of the good
That noble-minded Titus means to thee! 215
   Titus. Content thee, prince! I will restore to thee
The people's hearts and wean them from themselves.
   Bass. Andronicus, I do not flatter thee,
But honor thee, and will do till I die.
My faction if thou strengthen with thy friends, 220
I will most thankful be; and thanks to men
Of noble minds is honorable meed.
   Titus. People of Rome, and people's Tribunes here,
I ask your voices and your suffrages.
Will ye bestow them friendly on Andronicus? 225

227. **gratulate:** congratulate.

232. **Titan:** a name for the sun-god, Hyperion.

242. **in part:** in partial payment.

243. **gentleness:** courtesy.

248. **Pantheon:** a temple erected by Agrippa, later rebuilt by Hadrian, and now a Christian church called Santa Maria della Rotunda.

249. **motion:** suggestion.

251. **hold me:** regard myself.

Trib. To gratify the good Andronicus,
And gratulate his safe return to Rome,
The people will accept whom he admits.

    Titus. Tribune, I thank you; and this suit I make,
That you create our Emperor's eldest son,   230
Lord Saturnine; whose virtues will, I hope,
Reflect on Rome as Titan's rays on earth
And ripen justice in this commonweal.
Then, if you will elect by my advice,
Crown him, and say, "Long live our Emperor!"   235

    Mar. With voices and applause of every sort,
Patricians and plebeians, we create
Lord Saturninus Rome's great Emperor,
And say, "Long live our Emperor Saturnine!"
                  A long flourish till they come down.

    Sat. Titus Andronicus, for thy favors done   240
To us in our election this day,
I give thee thanks in part of thy deserts
And will with deeds requite thy gentleness;
And, for an onset, Titus, to advance
Thy name and honorable family,   245
Lavinia will I make my Empress,
Rome's royal mistress, mistress of my heart,
And in the sacred Pantheon her espouse.
Tell me, Andronicus, doth this motion please thee?

    Titus. It doth, my worthy lord; and in this match   250
I hold me highly honored of your Grace;
And here, in sight of Rome, to Saturnine,
King and commander of our commonweal,
The wide world's Emperor, do I consecrate
My sword, my chariot, and my prisoners,   255

256. **imperious:** imperial.

258. **ensigns:** symbols.

260. **proud . . . of:** highly gratified by.

268. **hue:** appearance.

272. **cheer:** expression.

277. **Can:** who can.

279. **sith:** since.

280. **Warrants:** justifies.

DONNE ILLVSTRI STOLLATE.

A Roman lady of noble birth. From Cesare Vecellio, *Habiti antichi et moderni di tutto il mondo* (1590).

11

Presents well worthy Rome's imperious lord.
Receive them, then, the tribute that I owe,
Mine honor's ensigns humbled at thy feet.

Sat. Thanks, noble Titus, father of my life!
How proud I am of thee and of thy gifts   260
Rome shall record; and when I do forget
The least of these unspeakable deserts,
Romans, forget your fealty to me.

Titus. [*To Tamora*] Now, madam, are you prisoner
to an emperor,   265
To him that, for your honor and your state,
Will use you nobly and your followers.

Sat. [*Aside*] A goodly lady, trust me, of the hue
That I would choose, were I to choose anew.—
Clear up, fair Queen, that cloudy countenance.   270
Though chance of war hath wrought this change of
cheer,
Thou comest not to be made a scorn in Rome.
Princely shall be thy usage every way.
Rest on my word, and let not discontent   275
Daunt all your hopes. Madam, he comforts you
Can make you greater than the Queen of Goths.—
Lavinia, you are not displeased with this?

Lav. Not I, my lord, sith true nobility
Warrants these words in princely courtesy.   280

Sat. Thanks, sweet Lavinia. Romans, let us go.
Ransomless here we set our prisoners free.
Proclaim our honors, lords, with trump and drum.
[*Flourish. Saturninus courts Tamora in dumb show.*]

Bass. [*Seizing Lavinia*] Lord Titus, by your leave,
this maid is mine.   285

288. **this reason and this right:** i.e., this right that is sanctioned by reason.

289. **Suum cuique:** to each his own.

294. **surprised:** captured.

Titus. How sir! are you in earnest, then, my lord?

Bass. Ay, noble Titus, and resolved withal
To do myself this reason and this right.

Mar. Suum cuique is our Roman justice.
This prince in justice seizeth but his own.   290

Luc. And that he will, and shall, if Lucius live.

Titus. Traitors, avaunt! Where is the Emperor's
    guard?
Treason, my lord! Lavinia is surprised!

Sat. Surprised! by whom?   295

Bass.   By him that justly may
Bear his betrothed from all the world away.

      [*Exeunt Bassianus and Marcus with Lavinia.*]

Mut. Brothers, help to convey her hence away,
And with my sword I'll keep this door safe.

      [*Exeunt Lucius, Quintus, and Martius.*]

Titus. Follow, my lord, and I'll soon bring her back. 300

Mut. My lord, you pass not here.

Titus.   What, villain boy!
Barrst me my way in Rome?

Mut.   Help, Lucius, help! *He kills him.*

[*During the fray, Saturninus, Tamora, Demetrius,
   Chiron, and Aaron go out, and re-enter above.*]

[*Enter Lucius.*]

Luc. My lord, you are unjust; and, more than so,   305
In wrongful quarrel you have slain your son.

Titus. Nor thou, nor he, are any sons of mine:
My sons would never so dishonor me.

314. by leisure: i.e., in his own sweet time; not readily, if ever.

317. stale: butt; laughingstock.

323. changing piece: false wench, who, like a coin, passes from hand to hand.

326. bandy: brawl.

327. ruffle: cause tumults.

330. Phoebe: another name for Diana, the moon-goddess.

331. gallant'st: loveliest.

339. Hymenaeus: the god who officiated at marriage rites.

Hymen, god of marriage. From Vincenzo Cartari, *Le imagini de gli dei de gli antichi* (1609).

Traitor, restore Lavinia to the Emperor.

   Luc. Dead, if you will, but not to be his wife   310
That is another's lawful promised love.   [*Exit.*]

   Sat. No, Titus, no: the Emperor needs her not,
Nor her, nor thee, nor any of thy stock.
I'll trust by leisure him that mocks me once;
Thee never, nor thy traitorous haughty sons,   315
Confederates all thus to dishonor me.
Was none in Rome to make a stale
But Saturnine? Full well, Andronicus,
Agree these deeds with that proud brag of thine
That saidst I begged the empire at thy hands.   320

   Titus. Oh, monstrous! what reproachful words are
     these?

   Sat. But go thy ways! Go, give that changing piece
To him that flourished for her with his sword.
A valiant son-in-law thou shalt enjoy,   325
One fit to bandy with thy lawless sons,
To ruffle in the commonwealth of Rome.

   Titus. These words are razors to my wounded heart.

   Sat. And therefore, lovely Tamora, Queen of Goths,
That, like the stately Phoebe 'mongst her nymphs,   330
Dost overshine the gallant'st dames of Rome,
If thou be pleased with this my sudden choice,
Behold, I choose thee, Tamora, for my bride
And will create thee Empress of Rome.
Speak, Queen of Goths, dost thou applaud my choice? 335
And here I swear by all the Roman gods,
Sith priest and holy water are so near,
And tapers burn so bright, and everything
In readiness for Hymenaeus stand,

355. challenged: accused.

I will not re-salute the streets of Rome,   340
Or climb my palace, till from forth this place
I lead espoused my bride along with me.
   Tam. And here in sight of Heaven to Rome I swear,
If Saturnine advance the Queen of Goths,
She will a handmaid be to his desires,   345
A loving nurse, a mother to his youth.
   Sat. Ascend, fair Queen, Pantheon. Lords, accompany
     pany
Your noble Emperor and his lovely bride,
Sent by the Heavens for Prince Saturnine,   350
Whose wisdom hath her fortune conquered.
There shall we consummate our spousal rites.
                Exeunt [all but Titus].
   Titus. I am not bid to wait upon this bride.
Titus, when wert thou wont to walk alone,
Dishonored thus and challenged of wrongs?   355

Enter Marcus and Titus' sons, [Lucius, Quintus, and Martius].

   Mar. O Titus, see, oh, see what thou hast done!
In a bad quarrel slain a virtuous son.
   Titus. No, foolish Tribune, no! No son of mine,
Nor thou, nor these, confederates in the deed
That hath dishonored all our family: 360
Unworthy brother and unworthy sons!
   Luc. But let us give him burial, as becomes;
Give Mutius burial with our brethren.
   Titus. Traitors, away! He rests not in this tomb.
This monument five hundred years hath stood,   365

366. **re-edified:** rebuilt.

367. **servitors:** servants.

376. **vouch:** confirm.

377. **in my despite:** in spite of me.

380. **struck upon my crest:** i.e., battered the insignia of my honor.

384. **not with himself:** not himself.

389. **if all the rest will speed:** the meaning may be "if you ever expect to influence me by your speech in future."

Which I have sumptuously re-edified.
Here none but soldiers and Rome's servitors
Repose in fame, none basely slain in brawls.
Bury him where you can, he comes not here.

 Mar. My lord, this is impiety in you. 370
My nephew Mutius' deeds do plead for him:
He must be buried with his brethren.

 Quin., Mart. And shall, or him we will accompany.

 Titus. And shall! What villain was it spake that
  word? 375

 Quin. He that would vouch it in any place but here.

 Titus. What, would you bury him in my despite?

 Mar. No, noble Titus, but entreat of thee
To pardon Mutius and to bury him.

 Titus. Marcus, even thou hast struck upon my crest, 380
And with these boys mine honor thou hast wounded.
My foes I do repute you every one;
So trouble me no more, but get you gone.

 Mart. He is not with himself: let us withdraw.

 Quin. Not I, till Mutius' bones be buried. 385
     The brother and the sons kneel.

 Mar. Brother, for in that name doth Nature plead—

 Quin. Father, and in that name doth Nature
  speak—

 Titus Speak thou no more, if all the rest will speed.

 Mar. Renowned Titus, more than half my soul— 390

 Luc. Dear father, soul and substance of us all—

 Mar. Suffer thy brother Marcus to inter
His noble nephew here in virtue's nest,
That died in honor and Lavinia's cause.
Thou art a Roman: be not barbarous. 395

396. **advice:** deliberation; **Ajax:** the son of Telamon, who went mad and killed himself when Achilles' armor was awarded to Ulysses.

397. **Laertes' son:** Ulysses, who persuaded the Greeks to give Ajax decent burial.

407. **trophies:** memorials.

412. **subtle:** crafty.

415. **device:** stratagem; trickery.

The Greeks upon advice did bury Ajax
That slew himself; and wise Laertes' son
Did graciously plead for his funerals.
Let not young Mutius, then, that was thy joy,
Be barred his entrance here.   400
    Titus.   Rise, Marcus, rise.
                                                [*They rise.*]
The dismall'st day is this that e'er I saw,
To be dishonored by my sons in Rome!
Well, bury him, and bury me the next.
                                They put him in the tomb.
    Luc. There lie thy bones, sweet Mutius, with thy   405
        friends,
Till we with trophies do adorn thy tomb.
    All. [*Kneeling*] No man shed tears for noble
        Mutius:
He lives in fame that died in virtue's cause.   410
    Mar. My lord, to step out of these dreary dumps,
How comes it that the subtle Queen of Goths
Is of a sudden thus advanced in Rome?
    Titus. I know not, Marcus; but I know it is,
Whether by device or no, the Heavens can tell.   415
Is she not then beholding to the man
That brought her for this high good turn so far?
Yes, and will nobly him remunerate.

Flourish. Enter the Emperor [*Saturninus,*] *Tamora, and
her two sons,* [*Demetrius, Chiron,*] *with the Moor
[Aaron] at one door. Enter at the other door Bassianus
and Lavinia, with others.*

419. **played your prize:** won your game.

428. **that:** that which.

436. **in opinion and in honor:** in honorable reputation.

440. **frankly:** freely.

444. **leave:** cease.

Sat. So, Bassianus, you have played your prize.
God give you joy, sir, of your gallant bride!   420

Bass. And you of yours, my lord! I say no more,
Nor wish no less; and so I take my leave.

Sat. Traitor, if Rome have law, or we have power,
Thou and thy faction shall repent this rape.

Bass. Rape, call you it, my lord, to seize my own,   425
My true-betrothed love, and now my wife?
But let the laws of Rome determine all:
Meanwhile am I possessed of that is mine.

Sat. 'Tis good, sir. You are very short with us;
But if we live we'll be as sharp with you.   430

Bass. My lord, what I have done, as best I may,
Answer I must, and shall do with my life.
Only thus much I give your Grace to know:
By all the duties that I owe to Rome,
This noble gentleman, Lord Titus here,   435
Is in opinion and in honor wronged,
That, in the rescue of Lavinia,
With his own hand did slay his youngest son,
In zeal to you and highly moved to wrath
To be controlled in that he frankly gave.   440
Receive him then to favor, Saturnine,
That hath expressed himself in all his deeds
A father and a friend to thee and Rome.

Titus. Prince Bassianus, leave to plead my deeds.
'Tis thou and those that have dishonored me.   445
Rome and the righteous heavens be my judge
How I have loved and honored Saturnine!

Tam. My worthy lord, if ever Tamora
Were gracious in those princely eyes of thine,

450. **indifferently:** without prejudice.

453. **put it up:** put up with it.

454. **forfend:** forbid.

455. **author:** agent.

456. **undertake:** vouch.

460. **vain suppose:** idle supposition.

464. **griefs:** grievances.

467. **Upon a just survey:** after honest deliberation.

470. **at entreats:** to entreaties; **let me alone:** allow me to deal with the matter.

Then hear me speak indifferently for all;   450
And at my suit, sweet, pardon what is past.
  Sat. What, madam! be dishonored openly,
And basely put it up without revenge?
  Tam. Not so, my lord: the gods of Rome forfend
I should be author to dishonor you!   455
But on mine honor dare I undertake
For good Lord Titus' innocence in all;
Whose fury not dissembled speaks his griefs.
Then, at my suit, look graciously on him;
Lose not so noble a friend on vain suppose,   460
Nor with sour looks afflict his gentle heart.
[*Aside to Saturninus*] My lord, be ruled by me, be
    won at last;
Dissemble all your griefs and discontents.
You are but newly planted in your throne;   465
Lest then the people, and patricians too,
Upon a just survey, take Titus' part,
And so supplant you for ingratitude,
Which Rome reputes to be a heinous sin,
Yield at entreats, and then let me alone.   470
I'll find a day to massacre them all,
And raze their faction and their family,
The cruel father and his traitorous sons,
To whom I sued for my dear son's life;
And make them know what 'tis to let a queen   475
Kneel in the streets and beg for grace in vain.—
Come, come, sweet Emperor—come, Andronicus—
Take up this good old man, and cheer the heart
That dies in tempest of thy angry frown.
  Sat. Rise, Titus, rise! My empress hath prevailed. 480

483. incorporate in: i.e., made one with.
498. Tend'ring: having a care for.
511. part: depart.

Titus. I thank your Majesty, and her, my lord.
These words, these looks, infuse new life in me.
  Tam. Titus, I am incorporate in Rome,
A Roman now adopted happily,
And must advise the Emperor for his good.   485
This day all quarrels die, Andronicus.
And let it be mine honor, good my lord,
That I have reconciled your friends and you.
For you, Prince Bassianus, I have passed
My word and promise to the Emperor   490
That you will be more mild and tractable.
And fear not, lords, and you, Lavinia:
By my advice, all humbled on your knees,
You shall ask pardon of His Majesty.
  Luc. We do, and vow to Heaven and to His   495
    Highness
That what we did was mildly as we might,
Tend'ring our sister's honor and our own.
  Mar. That, on mine honor, here do I protest.
  Sat. Away, and talk not: trouble us no more.   500
  Tam. Nay, nay, sweet Emperor, we must all be
    friends.
The Tribune and his nephews kneel for grace:
I will not be denied. Sweetheart, look back.
  Sat. Marcus, for thy sake and thy brother's here, 505
And at my lovely Tamora's entreats,
I do remit these young men's heinous faults.
Stand up.
Lavinia, though you left me like a churl,
I found a friend; and sure as death I swore   510
I would not part a bachelor from the priest.

515. **and:** if.

517. **give . . . bonjour:** i.e., greet with a morning serenade.

518. **gramercy:** many thanks.

Come, if the Emperor's court can feast two brides,
You are my guest, Lavinia, and your friends.
This day shall be a love-day, Tamora.

    Titus. Tomorrow, and it please your Majesty   515
To hunt the panther and the hart with me,
With horn and hound we'll give your Grace bonjour.

    Sat. Be it so, Titus, and gramercy too.

                Exeunt. Sound trumpets.

TITUS
ANDRONICUS

ACT II

II. [i.] Aaron, a Moor, lover of Tamora, gloats over her fortunate position and his dominance of her; he sees a golden future for himself. Tamora's sons, Chiron and Demetrius, wrangle over which of them will win the favor of Lavinia, whom both desire. Aaron suggests that the forest offers many secluded spots where Lavinia may be raped and urges them to seek their mother's advice as to the best plan to achieve their desire.

7. **zodiac:** circuit of the heavens.

8. **overlooks:** looks down upon; **peering:** towering.

10. **wit:** wisdom.

14. **pitch:** height.

17. **Prometheus:** punished by Zeus for his rebellion in giving fire to mankind.

18. **weeds:** garments.

Prometheus bound to a peak in the Caucasus. From Geoffrey Whitney, *A Choice of Emblems* (1586).

ACT II

[Scene I. Rome. Before the palace.]

Enter Aaron.

Aar. Now climbeth Tamora Olympus' top,
Safe out of Fortune's shot, and sits aloft,
Secure of thunder's crack or lightning flash,
Advanced above pale envy's threat'ning reach.
As when the golden sun salutes the morn,   5
And, having gilt the ocean with his beams,
Gallops the zodiac in his glistering coach,
And overlooks the highest peering hills,
So Tamora.
Upon her wit doth earthly honor wait,   10
And virtue stoops and trembles at her frown.
Then, Aaron, arm thy heart and fit thy thoughts,
To mount aloft with thy imperial mistress,
And mount her pitch, whom thou in triumph long
Hast prisoner held, fettered in amorous chains,   15
And faster bound to Aaron's charming eyes
Than is Prometheus tied to Caucasus.
Away with slavish weeds and servile thoughts!
I will be bright and shine in pearl and gold,

22. **Semiramis:** wife of King Ninus of Assyria, famous for her beauty and lasciviousness.

SD 25. **braving:** threatening each other.

26. **wants:** lacks.

28. **graced:** favored.

29. **affected be:** be preferred.

30. **overween:** presume.

31. **braves:** challenges.

33. **gracious:** pleasing.

36. **approve:** demonstrate.

38. **Clubs:** in Elizabethan London, a rallying cry for the watch, armed with clubs, to quell a riot.

40. **unadvised:** unwisely.

41. **dancing-rapier:** a light sword worn for decorative purposes on social occasions.

43. **lath:** sword made of lath, such as were used by actors.

Semiramis. From *Le microcosme, contenant divers tableaux de la vie humaine* (n.d.).

To wait upon this new-made Empress.   20
To wait, said I? To wanton with this queen,
This goddess, this Semiramis, this nymph,
This siren, that will charm Rome's Saturnine
And see his shipwrack and his commonweal's.
Holloa! what storm is this?   25

Enter Chiron and Demetrius, braving.

   Dem. Chiron, thy years wants wit, thy wits wants
     edge
And manners, to intrude where I am graced
And may, for aught thou knowest, affected be.
   Chir. Demetrius, thou dost overween in all,   30
And so in this, to bear me down with braves.
'Tis not the difference of a year or two
Makes me less gracious or thee more fortunate.
I am as able and as fit as thou
To serve and to deserve my mistress' grace;   35
And that my sword upon thee shall approve,
And plead my passions for Lavinia's love.
   Aar. [*Aside*] Clubs, clubs! These lovers will not
     keep the peace.
   Dem. Why, boy, although our mother, unadvised,   40
Gave you a dancing-rapier by your side,
Are you so desperate grown to threat your friends?
Go to! Have your lath glued within your sheath
Till you know better how to handle it.
   Chir. Meanwhile, sir, with the little skill I have,   45
Full well shalt thou perceive how much I dare.
   Dem. Ay, boy, grow ye so brave?   *They draw.*

51. **wot:** know.
66. **brabble:** brawl.
68. **jet:** encroach.
71. **broached:** initiated.
74. **ground:** foundation, with a pun on the musical sense.
77. **meaner:** baser; less noble.

   Aar. [*Coming forward*]   Why, how now, lords!
So near the Emperor's palace dare ye draw
And maintain such a quarrel openly?   50
Full well I wot the ground of all this grudge.
I would not for a million of gold
The cause were known to them it most concerns;
Nor would your noble mother for much more
Be so dishonored in the court of Rome.   55
For shame, put up.
   Dem.   Not I, till I have sheathed
My rapier in his bosom and withal
Thrust those reproachful speeches down his throat
That he hath breathed in my dishonor here.   60
   Chir. For that I am prepared and full resolved.
Foul-spoken coward! that thunderst with thy tongue,
And with thy weapon nothing darest perform.
   Aar. Away, I say!
Now, by the gods that warlike Goths adore,   65
This petty brabble will undo us all.
Why, lords, and think you not how dangerous
It is to jet upon a prince's right?
What, is Lavinia then become so loose,
Or Bassianus so degenerate,   70
That for her love such quarrels may be broached
Without controlment, justice, or revenge?
Young lords, beware! and should the Empress know
This discord's ground, the music would not please.
   Chir. I care not, I, knew she and all the world.   75
I love Lavinia more than all the world.
   Dem. Youngling, learn thou to make some meaner
     choice.

82. **brook:** put up with.

94. **shive:** slice.

96. **Vulcan's badge:** the horns attributed to the cuckold (referring to the unfaithfulness of Vulcan's wife, Venus).

99. **court it:** act the wooer.

100. **liberality:** generosity.

103. **snatch:** taste.

105. **so the turn were served:** i.e., provided each of us were satisfied in turn.

107. **hit it:** Aaron's reply puns on a bawdy sense of the phrase referring to sexual achievement.

Fame, in a mantle covered with eyes and ears. From Cesare Ripa, *Iconologie* (1677). (See l. 138.)

Lavinia is thine elder brother's hope.

Aar. Why, are ye mad? or know ye not in Rome   80
How furious and impatient they be,
And cannot brook competitors in love?
I tell you, lords, you do but plot your deaths
By this device.

Chir.   Aaron, a thousand deaths   85
Would I propose to achieve her whom I love.

Aar. To achieve her! how?

Dem.   Why makes thou it so strange?
She is a woman, therefore may be wooed;
She is a woman, therefore may be won;   90
She is Lavinia, therefore must be loved.
What, man! more water glideth by the mill
Than wots the miller of; and easy it is
Of a cut loaf to steal a shive, we know.
Though Bassianus be the Emperor's brother,   95
Better than he have worn Vulcan's badge.

Aar. [*Aside*] Ay, and as good as Saturninus may.

Dem. Then why should he despair that knows to
          court it
With words, fair looks, and liberality?   100
What, hast not thou full often struck a doe
And borne her cleanly by the keeper's nose?

Aar. Why, then, it seems, some certain snatch or so
Would serve your turns.

Chir.   Ay, so the turn were served.   105

Dem. Aaron, thou hast hit it.

Aar.   Would you had hit it too!
Then should not we be tired with this ado.
Why, hark ye, hark ye! and are you such fools

110. **square:** quarrel.

111. **speed:** succeed.

115. **jar:** dispute.

116. **policy and stratagem:** crafty trick.

117. **affect:** desire.

119. **perforce:** willy-nilly; **as you may:** echoing the proverb "Men must do as they may, not as they would."

120. **Lucrece:** the Roman matron whom Tarquin ravished, the subject of Shakespeare's narrative poem *The Rape of Lucrece*.

124. **solemn:** formal and ceremonious.

128. **by kind:** naturally.

129. **Single:** draw apart.

130. **strike her home:** conquer her.

132. **sacred:** dedicated. The adjective merely serves to emphasize the idea that her intelligence is wholly intent upon **villainy and vengeance.**

133. **villainy and vengeance:** vengeful mischief.

135. **file:** sharpen; **engines:** ingenuity.

136. **square yourselves:** i.e., work at cross purposes to thwart each other.

138. **Fame:** the personification of rumor.

To square for this? Would it offend you, then,   110
That both should speed?
  Chir. Faith, not me.
  Dem.   Nor me, so I were one.
  Aar. For shame, be friends, and join for that you
      jar.   115
'Tis policy and stratagem must do
That you affect; and so much you resolve,
That what you cannot as you would achieve,
You must perforce accomplish as you may.
Take this of me: Lucrece was not more chaste   120
Than this Lavinia, Bassianus' love.
A speedier course than ling'ring languishment
Must we pursue, and I have found the path.
My lords, a solemn hunting is in hand:
There will the lovely Roman ladies troop.   125
The forest walks are wide and spacious;
And many unfrequented plots there are
Fitted by kind for rape and villainy.
Single you thither then this dainty doe,
And strike her home by force if not by words.   130
This way, or not at all, stand you in hope.
Come, come, our Empress, with her sacred wit
To villainy and vengeance consecrate,
Will we acquaint withal what we intend;
And she shall file our engines with advice   135
That will not suffer you to square yourselves
But to your wishes' height advance you both.
The Emperor's court is like the house of Fame,
The palace full of tongues, of eyes and ears.
The woods are ruthless, dreadful, deaf, and dull: 140

146. **Sit fas aut nefas:** whether it be right or wrong.

148. **Per Styga, per manes vehor:** "through Stygia and the shades I am carried" (i.e., I suffer the tortures of hell), apparently a slight rephrasing of Phaedra's words in Seneca's *Phaedra* 1180.

▬▬▬▬▬▬▬▬▬▬▬

II. [ii.] Titus prepares for the hunt. Saturninus is ungracious at being roused so early, but the Andronici promise good sport. Tamora's sons are filled with anticipation of the prey they hope to capture.

▬▬▬▬▬▬▬

1. **up:** under way; **gay:** the Quarto and Folio read "gray," which commentators have explained as characterizing the cold light of early morning, but "gray" may be simply a typographical error.

3. **make a bay:** cause the dogs to bay.

7. **charge:** responsibility.

There speak, and strike, brave boys, and take your
    turns;
There serve your lust, shadowed from Heaven's eye,
And revel in Lavinia's treasury.

   Chir. Thy counsel, lad, smells of no cowardice.   145

   Dem. Sit fas aut nefas, till I find the stream
To cool this heat, a charm to calm these fits,
Per Styga, per manes vehor.

                                   Exeunt.

Scene II.   [A forest near Rome.]

*Enter Titus Andronicus and his three sons, making a
noise with hounds and horns; and Marcus.*

   Titus. The hunt is up, the morn is bright and gay,
The fields are fragrant, and the woods are green.
Uncouple here, and let us make a bay,
And wake the Emperor and his lovely bride,
And rouse the Prince, and ring a hunter's peal,   5
That all the court may echo with the noise.
Sons, let it be your charge, as it is ours,
To attend the Emperor's person carefully.
I have been troubled in my sleep this night,
But dawning day new comfort hath inspired.   10

*Here a cry of hounds, and wind horns in a peal. Then
enter Saturninus, Tamora, Bassianus, Lavinia, Chiron,
Demetrius, and their Attendants.*

24. **proudest:** most spirited; **chase:** field.
27. **Makes way:** runs before it.

▬▬▬▬▬▬▬▬▬▬▬▬▬▬▬

II. [iii.] Aaron, carrying out Tamora's plot, buries gold. When Tamora greets him amorously, he declares that his mind is occupied with vengeance. The day will see the death of Bassianus and Lavinia's rape and mutilation. These unsuspecting victims taunt Tamora about her illicit love for Aaron. In retaliation, Tamora falsely accuses them of threatening her, and Demetrius and Chiron stab Bassianus. Tamora's move to kill Lavinia is stopped by Demetrius, who tells her that they have other plans. When Lavinia realizes what they have in mind, she pleads with Tamora to show mercy by killing her at once. Tamora reminds her sons that Titus rejected her plea for her own son's life; they will best please her by giving Lavinia the worst possible treatment. Demetrius throws Bassianus' body into a nearby pit, and he and Chiron drag Lavinia away. Aaron has lured Titus' sons to the spot and Martius falls into the pit. Quintus attempts to rescue his brother but falls in too, just as Aaron reappears with Saturninus. Tamora also arrives, with Titus. She gives Saturninus a letter that Titus has found, which reveals a plan to murder Bassianus; it mentions buried gold for the murderer's fee. This forgery by Aaron is accepted by Saturninus as proving the guilt of Titus' sons. He refuses Titus' petition to let them be bailed, and Martius and Quintus are dragged off as prisoners.

▬▬▬▬▬▬▬▬▬▬

1. **wit:** sense.
3. **inherit:** possess.

Many good morrows to your Majesty;
Madam, to you as many and as good.
I promised your Grace a hunter's peal.
   Sat. And you have rung it lustily, my lords,
Somewhat too early for new-married ladies.   15
   Bass. Lavinia, how say you?
   Lav.   I say no:
I have been broad awake two hours and more.
   Sat. Come on then: horse and chariots let us have,
And to our sport. [*To Tamora*] Madam, now shall ye   20
    see
Our Roman hunting.
   Mar.   I have dogs, my lord,
Will rouse the proudest panther in the chase
And climb the highest promontory top.   25
   Titus. And I have horse will follow where the game
Makes way, and runs like swallows o'er the plain.
   Dem. Chiron, we hunt not, we, with horse nor
    hound,
But hope to pluck a dainty doe to ground.   30
                                     Exeunt.

Scene III.   [A lonely part of the forest.]

Enter Aaron alone, [with a bag of gold].

   Aar. He that had wit would think that I had none,
To bury so much gold under a tree,
And never after to inherit it.

4. **abjectly:** contemptuously.

9. **have their alms out of the Empress' chest:**
i.e., find the gold, which Tamora has supplied for
the purpose.

11. **boast:** show.

20. **yellowing:** a form of "yelling"; cf. bellowing.

21. **conflict:** i.e., amorous encounter.

22. **wand'ring prince:** Aeneas.

23. **happy:** opportune; **surprised:** overtaken.
Aeneas and Dido first became lovers when they took
shelter in a cave from a sudden storm (Vergil,
Aeneid, bk. iv).

Sign for the planet Saturn. From Abū Ma'shar, *Albumasar de
magnis junctionis* (1515). (See l. 31.)

Let him that thinks of me so abjectly
Know that this gold must coin a stratagem,   5
Which, cunningly effected, will beget
A very excellent piece of villainy:
And so repose, sweet gold, for their unrest
                                   [*Hides the gold.*]
That have their alms out of the Empress' chest.

Enter Tamora, alone, to the Moor.

Tam. My lovely Aaron, wherefore lookst thou sad   10
When everything doth make a gleeful boast?
The birds chant melody on every bush;
The snake lies rolled in the cheerful sun;
The green leaves quiver with the cooling wind
And make a chequered shadow on the ground.   15
Under their sweet shade, Aaron, let us sit,
And, whilst the babbling echo mocks the hounds,
Replying shrilly to the well-tuned horns,
As if a double hunt were heard at once,
Let us sit down and mark their yellowing noise;   20
And, after conflict such as was supposed
The wand'ring prince and Dido once enjoyed,
When with a happy storm they were surprised
And curtained with a counsel-keeping cave,
We may, each wreathed in the other's arms,   25
Our pastimes done, possess a golden slumber,
Whiles hounds and horns and sweet melodious birds
Be unto us as is a nurse's song
Of lullaby to bring her babe asleep.

Aar. Madam, though Venus govern your desires,   30

31. Saturn: the planet whose influence produced a taciturn and menacing disposition.

32. deadly-standing: i.e., possessing a death-dealing stare, like the mythical basilisk.

37. venereal: amorous.

39. Blood and revenge: bloody revenge.

43. Philomel: Philomela inspired the lust of her brother-in-law, Tereus, who ravished her and cut out her tongue so that she could not accuse him (Ovid, *Metamorphoses*, bk. vi).

47. fatal-plotted: planned to have fatal effect.

53. cross: quarrelsome.

56. well-beseeming: suitably becoming, in terms of decorum.

57. habited: clothed.

Diana, the moon-goddess. From Vincenzo Cartari, *Imagini de gli dei delli antichi* (1615).

Saturn is dominator over mine.
What signifies my deadly-standing eye,
My silence, and my cloudy melancholy,
My fleece of woolly hair that now uncurls
Even as an adder when she doth unroll   35
To do some fatal execution?
No, madam, these are no venereal signs:
Vengeance is in my heart, death in my hand,
Blood and revenge are hammering in my head.
Hark, Tamora, the empress of my soul,   40
Which never hopes more Heaven than rests in thee,
This is the day of doom for Bassianus:
His Philomel must lose her tongue today,
Thy sons make pillage of her chastity
And wash their hands in Bassianus' blood.   45
Seest thou this letter? Take it up, I pray thee,
And give the King this fatal-plotted scroll.
Now question me no more: we are espied.
Here comes a parcel of our hopeful booty,
Which dreads not yet their lives' destruction.   50

Enter Bassianus and Lavinia.

  Tam. Ah, my sweet Moor, sweeter to me than life!
  Aar. No more, great Empress: Bassianus comes.
Be cross with him, and I'll go fetch thy sons
To back thy quarrels, whatsoe'er they be.   [*Exit.*]
  Bass. Who have we here? Rome's royal Empress,   55
Unfurnished of her well-beseeming troop?
Or is it Dian, habited like her,
Who hath abandoned her holy groves

62. **presently:** immediately.

63. **Actaeon:** a hunter who spied on Diana bathing; she punished him by causing horns to sprout from his forehead, so that his dogs turned upon him and devoured him as though he were a deer.

66. **Under your patience:** if you will excuse my saying so.

67. **horning:** cuckolding your husband.

68. **to be doubted:** it is to be suspected.

72. **Cimmerian:** in Homer the Cimmerians were a people who dwelt in a land without sunlight, hence the word came to be used to characterize extreme darkness.

77. **obscure:** dark.

81. **rated:** scolded.

83. **joy:** enjoy.

84. **passing:** surpassingly.

85. **note:** notice.

86. **noted:** defamed.

87. **abused:** deceived.

Actaeon. From Henry Peacham, *Minerva Britanna* (1612).

To see the general hunting in this forest?

   Tam. Saucy controller of my private steps!   60
Had I the pow'r that some say Dian had,
Thy temples should be planted presently
With horns, as was Actaeon's, and the hounds
Should drive upon thy new-transformed limbs,
Unmannerly intruder as thou art!   65

   Lav. Under your patience, gentle Empress,
'Tis thought you have a goodly gift in horning;
And to be doubted that your Moor and you
Are singled forth to try experiments.
Jove shield your husband from his hounds today!   70
'Tis pity they should take him for a stag.

   Bass. Believe me, Queen, your swarthy Cimmerian
Doth make your honor of his body's hue,
Spotted, detested, and abominable.
Why are you sequest'red from all your train,   75
Dismounted from your snow-white goodly steed,
And wandered hither to an obscure plot,
Accompanied but with a barbarous Moor,
If foul desire had not conducted you?

   Lav. And, being intercepted in your sport,   80
Great reason that my noble lord be rated
For sauciness.—I pray you, let us hence,
And let her joy her raven-colored love:
This valley fits the purpose passing well.

   Bass. The King my brother shall have note of this.   85

   Lav. Ay, for these slips have made him noted long:
Good king, to be so mightily abused!

   Tam. Why, I have patience to endure all this.

98. **fatal raven:** the raven was considered a bird of ill omen.

102. **urchins:** hedgehogs, often considered to be evil spirits in animal shape.

103. **fearful and confused:** causing such fear as to confound sanity.

105. **straight:** at once.

Enter Chiron and Demetrius.

Dem. How now, dear sovereign and our gracious
    mother!   90
Why doth your Highness look so pale and wan?
Tam. Have I not reason, think you, to look pale?
These two have ticed me hither to this place.
A barren detested vale you see it is:
The trees, though summer, yet forlorn and lean,   95
Overcome with moss and baleful mistletoe.
Here never shines the sun; here nothing breeds,
Unless the nightly owl or fatal raven.
And when they showed me this abhorred pit,
They told me, here, at dead time of the night,   100
A thousand fiends, a thousand hissing snakes,
Ten thousand swelling toads, as many urchins,
Would make such fearful and confused cries,
As any mortal body hearing it
Should straight fall mad, or else die suddenly.   105
No sooner had they told this hellish tale,
But straight they told me they would bind me here
Unto the body of a dismal yew,
And leave me to this miserable death.
And then they called me foul adulteress,   110
Lascivious Goth, and all the bitterest terms
That ever ear did hear to such effect;
And had you not by wondrous fortune come
This vengeance on me had they executed.
Revenge it, as you love your mother's life,   115
Or be ye not henceforth called my children.

118. **home:** i.e., with fatal effect.

125. **Here is more belongs to her:** she has more coming to her than this.

127. **minion:** darling (contemptuously); **stood upon:** insisted upon.

129. **painted:** false.

137. **sure:** certain.

139. **nice-preserved:** fastidiously preserved; **honesty:** chastity.

Dem. This is a witness that I am thy son.

                       Stabs [Bassianus].

Chir. And this for me, struck home to show my
    strength.   [*Also stabs Bassianus, who dies.*]

Lav. Ay, come, Semiramis, nay, barbarous Tamora, 120
For no name fits thy nature but thy own!

Tam. Give me the poniard: you shall know, my
    boys,
Your mother's hand shall right your mother's wrong.

Dem. Stay, madam! Here is more belongs to her. 125
First thrash the corn, then after burn the straw:
This minion stood upon her chastity,
Upon her nuptial vow, her loyalty,
And with that painted hope braves your mightiness.
And shall she carry this unto her grave? 130

Chir. And if she do, I would I were an eunuch.
Drag hence her husband to some secret hole,
And make his dead trunk pillow to our lust.

Tam. But when ye have the honey ye desire,
Let not this wasp outlive us both to sting. 135

Chir. I warrant you, madam, we will make that
    sure.
Come, mistress, now perforce we will enjoy
That nice-preserved honesty of yours.

Lav. O Tamora! thou bearest a woman's face— 140

Tam. I will not hear her speak. Away with her!

Lav. Sweet lords, entreat her hear me but a word.

Dem. Listen, fair madam: let it be your glory
To see her tears, but be your heart to them
As unrelenting flint to drops of rain. 145

148. **learn:** teach.

150. **tyranny:** ferocity.

158. **The lion, moved with pity:** probably referring to the Aesop fable of the lion who fell in love with a beautiful girl and consented to the pulling of his teeth and paring of his claws in order to woo her.

163. **something:** somewhat.

Lav. When did the tiger's young ones teach the
    dam?
Oh, do not learn her wrath! She taught it thee:
The milk thou suckst from her did turn to marble.
Even at thy teat thou hadst thy tyranny.   150
Yet every mother breeds not sons alike.
[*To Chiron*] Do thou entreat her show a woman's
    pity.
  Chir. What, wouldst thou have me prove myself a
    bastard?   155
  Lav. 'Tis true: the raven doth not hatch a lark.
Yet have I heard,—Oh, could I find it now!—
The lion, moved with pity, did endure
To have his princely paws pared all away.
Some say that ravens foster forlorn children,   160
The whilst their own birds famish in their nests.
Oh, be to me, though thy hard heart say no,
Nothing so kind, but something pitiful!
  Tam. I know not what it means. Away with her!
  Lav. Oh, let me teach thee! For my father's sake,   165
That gave thee life, when well he might have slain
    thee,
Be not obdurate, open thy deaf ears.
  Tam. Hadst thou in person ne'er offended me,
Even for his sake am I pitiless.   170
Remember, boys, I poured forth tears in vain
To save your brother from the sacrifice;
But fierce Andronicus would not relent.
Therefore, away with her, and use her as you will;
The worse to her, the better loved of me.   175
  Lav. O Tamora, be called a gentle queen,

180. **Fond:** foolish.

183. **denies:** forbids.

193. **blot and enemy to:** discreditor of; **our general name:** i.e., the reputation of the whole female sex.

194. **Confusion:** destruction.

201. **made away:** slain.

203. **spleenful:** passionate.

And with thine own hands kill me in this place!
For 'tis not life that I have begged so long:
Poor I was slain when Bassianus died.

Tam. What beggst thou then? Fond woman, let me 180
go.

Lav. 'Tis present death I beg, and one thing more
That womanhood denies my tongue to tell.
Oh, keep me from their worse than killing lust,
And tumble me into some loathsome pit, 185
Where never man's eye may behold my body.
Do this, and be a charitable murderer.

Tam. So should I rob my sweet sons of their fee.
No, let them satisfy their lust on thee.

Dem. Away! for thou hast stayed us here too long. 190

Lav. No grace? No womanhood? Ah, beastly
creature!
The blot and enemy to our general name!
Confusion fall—

Chir. Nay, then I'll stop your mouth. Bring thou 195
her husband.
This is the hole where Aaron bid us hide him.

[*Demetrius throws the body of Bassianus into the pit;
then exeunt Demetrius and Chiron, dragging off
Lavinia.*]

Tam. Farewell, my sons: see that you make her
sure.
Ne'er let my heart know merry cheer indeed 200
Till all the Andronici be made away.
Now will I hence to seek my lovely Moor,
And let my spleenful sons this trull deflow'r. *Exit.*

204. **the better foot before:** a proverbial phrase, meaning to hasten.

211. **subtle:** cunning.

226. **surprised:** overcome; **uncouth:** unusual; eerie.

Enter Aaron, with [Quintus and Martius].

Aar. Come on, my lords, the better foot before.
Straight will I bring you to the loathsome pit   205
Where I espied the panther fast asleep.
  Quin. My sight is very dull, whate'er it bodes.
  Mart. And mine, I promise you: were it not for
    shame,
Well could I leave our sport to sleep awhile.   210
                      [Falls into the pit.]
  Quin. What, art thou fallen? What subtle hole is
    this,
Whose mouth is covered with rude-growing briers,
Upon whose leaves are drops of new-shed blood
As fresh as morning dew distilled on flowers?   215
A very fatal place it seems to me.
Speak, brother, hast thou hurt thee with the fall?
  Mart. O brother, with the dismal'st object hurt
That ever eye with sight made heart lament!
  Aar. *[Aside]* Now will I fetch the King to find them 220
    here,
That he thereby may have a likely guess
How these were they that made away his brother.
                              Exit.
  Mart. Why dost not comfort me and help me out
From this unhallowed and bloodstained hole?   225
  Quin. I am surprised with an uncouth fear;
A chilling sweat o'erruns my trembling joints;
My heart suspects more than mine eye can see.
  Mart. To prove thou hast a true-divining heart,

237. **imbrued:** steeped.

243. **monument:** tomb.

246. **Pyramus:** the lover of Thisbe, who killed himself when he mistakenly thought she had been devoured by a lion (Ovid, *Metamorphoses*, bk. iv).

249. **faint:** weak.

250. **fell:** deadly.

251. **Cocytus:** one of the rivers of Hades.

Thisbe kills herself on Pyramus' body. From Gabriele Simeoni, *La vita et Metamorfoseo d'Ovidio* (1559).

Aaron and thou look down into this den,   230
And see a fearful sight of blood and death.

   Quin. Aaron is gone, and my compassionate heart
Will not permit mine eyes once to behold
The thing whereat it trembles by surmise.
Oh, tell me who it is: for ne'er till now   235
Was I a child to fear I know not what.

   Mart. Lord Bassianus lies imbrued in blood,
All on a heap, like to a slaughtered lamb,
In this detested, dark, blood-drinking pit.

   Quin. If it be dark, how dost thou know 'tis he?   240

   Mart. Upon his bloody finger he doth wear
A precious ring, that lightens all this hole,
Which, like a taper in some monument,
Doth shine upon the dead man's earthy cheeks,
And shows the ragged entrails of this pit.   245
So pale did shine the moon on Pyramus
When he by night lay bathed in maiden blood.
O brother, help me with thy fainting hand—
If fear hath made thee faint, as me it hath—
Out of this fell devouring receptacle,   250
As hateful as Cocytus' misty mouth.

   Quin. Reach me thy hand, that I may help thee out;
Or, wanting strength to do thee so much good,
I may be plucked into the swallowing womb
Of this deep pit, poor Bassianus' grave.   255
I have no strength to pluck thee to the brink.

   Mart. Nor I no strength to climb without thy help.

   Quin. Thy hand once more: I will not loose again,
Till thou art here aloft or I below.

280. **writ:** writing.
281. **complot:** conspiracy; **timeless:** untimely.
282. **fold:** conceal.

Thou canst not come to me: I come to thee.   260

                                    Falls in.

Enter the Emperor [Saturninus] and Aaron the Moor.

   Sat. Along with me. I'll see what hole is here,
And what he is that now is leaped into it.
Say, who art thou that lately didst descend
Into this gaping hollow of the earth?
   Mart. The unhappy sons of old Andronicus,   265
Brought hither in a most unlucky hour,
To find thy brother Bassianus dead.
   Sat. My brother dead! I know thou dost but jest.
He and his lady both are at the lodge
Upon the north side of this pleasant chase: 270
'Tis not an hour since I left them there.
   Mart. We know not where you left them all alive;
But, out, alas! here have we found him dead.

*Enter Tamora, [with Attendants;] Titus Andronicus,
and Lucius.*

   Tam. Where is my lord the King?
   Sat. Here, Tamora, though grieved with killing   275
   grief.
   Tam. Where is thy brother Bassianus?
   Sat. Now to the bottom dost thou search my wound.
Poor Bassianus here lies murdered.
   Tam. Then all too late I bring this fatal writ,   280
The complot of this timeless tragedy;
And wonder greatly that man's face can fold

283. tyranny: violence.
284. miss: fail.
284–85. handsomely: handily.
292. purchase us: secure us as.
299. kind: nature.

In pleasing smiles such murderous tyranny.

She giveth Saturnine a letter.

  Sat. (Reads) "And if we miss to meet him hand-
    somely, 285
Sweet huntsman—Bassianus 'tis we mean—
Do thou so much as dig the grave for him.
Thou knowst our meaning. Look for thy reward
Among the nettles at the elder tree
Which overshades the mouth of that same pit 290
Where we decreed to bury Bassianus.
Do this and purchase us thy lasting friends."
O Tamora! was ever heard the like?
This is the pit, and this the elder tree.
Look, sirs, if you can find the huntsman out 295
That should have murdered Bassianus here.

  Aar. My gracious lord, here is the bag of gold.

  Sat. [*To Titus*] Two of thy whelps, fell curs of
    bloody kind,
Have here bereft my brother of his life. 300
Sirs, drag them from the pit unto the prison.
There let them bide until we have devised
Some never-heard-of torturing pain for them.

  Tam. What, are they in this pit? Oh, wondrous
    thing! 305
How easily murder is discovered!

  Titus. High Emperor, upon my feeble knee
I beg this boon, with tears not lightly shed,
That this fell fault of my accursed sons—
Accursed, if the faults be proved in them— 310

  Sat. If it be proved! You see it is apparent.
Who found this letter? Tamora, was it you?

315. **reverend:** reverenced.

━━━

II. [iv.] Demetrius and Chiron release the ravished Lavinia after cutting out her tongue and cutting off her hands so that she cannot reveal her ravishers. Marcus finds her and compares her state with that of the mythological Philomela.

━━━━━━━━━━━━━━━━━━━━━━━━━━━━━━━

1. **and if:** if.
3. **bewray:** reveal.
5. **scrowl:** scrawl, meaning both "gesture" and "write."

Tam. Andronicus himself did take it up.

Titus. I did, my lord. Yet let me be their bail:
For, by my father's reverend tomb I vow   315
They shall be ready at your Highness' will
To answer their suspicion with their lives.

Sat. Thou shalt not bail them. See thou follow me.
Some bring the murdered body, some the murderers.
Let them not speak a word: the guilt is plain;   320
For, by my soul, were there worse end than death,
That end upon them should be executed.

Tam. Andronicus, I will entreat the King.
Fear not thy sons; they shall do well enough.

Titus. Come, Lucius, come; stay not to talk with 325
them.

Exeunt.

[Scene IV.   Another part of the forest.]

*Enter the Empress' sons, with Lavinia, her hands cut
off, and her tongue cut out, and ravished.*

Dem. So, now go tell, and if thy tongue can speak,
Who 'twas that cut thy tongue and ravished thee.

Chir. Write down thy mind, bewray thy meaning so,
And if thy stumps will let thee play the scribe.

Dem. See how with signs and tokens she can scrowl. 5

Chir. Go home, call for sweet water, wash thy
hands.

Dem. She hath no tongue to call, nor hands to wash;

13. **Cousin:** a term of near kinship.

Tereus and Philomela. From Gabriele Simeoni, *La vita et Metamorfoseo d'Ovidio* (1559).

And so let's leave her to her silent walks.
   Chir. And 'twere my cause, I should go hang myself.   10
   Dem. If thou hadst hands to help thee knit the cord.
              Exeunt [Demetrius and Chiron].

Wind Horns. Enter Marcus, from hunting.

   Mar. Who is this? My niece, that flies away so fast!
Cousin, a word: where is your husband?
If I do dream, would all my wealth would wake me!
If I do wake, some planet strike me down,   15
That I may slumber an eternal sleep!
Speak, gentle niece, what stern ungentle hands
Hath lopped and hewed and made thy body bare
Of her two branches, those sweet ornaments
Whose circling shadows kings have sought to sleep in,   20
And might not gain so great a happiness
As half thy love? Why dost not speak to me?
Alas, a crimson river of warm blood,
Like to a bubbling fountain stirred with wind,
Doth rise and fall between thy rosed lips,   25
Coming and going with thy honey breath.
But, sure, some Tereus hath deflowered thee,
And, lest thou shouldst detect him, cut thy tongue.
Ah, now thou turnst away thy face for shame!
And, notwithstanding all this loss of blood,   30
As from a conduit with three issuing spouts,
Yet do thy cheeks look red as Titan's face
Blushing to be encountered with a cloud.
Shall I speak for thee? Shall I say 'tis so?
Oh, that I knew thy heart; and knew the beast,   35

37. Sorrow concealed, like an oven stopped: an echo of two proverbs, "Fire that's closest kept burns most of all," and "Grief pent up will break the heart."

40. tedious: requiring toilsome labor.

41. mean: means.

52. Cerberus: the watchdog of the underworld; **Thracian poet:** Orpheus charmed the underworld denizens with his music, when he visited Hades to beg for the return of his wife, Eurydice.

Orpheus and charmed animals. From Ovid, *Metamorphoses* (1509).

That I might rail at him to ease my mind!
Sorrow concealed, like an oven stopped,
Doth burn the heart to cinders where it is.
Fair Philomel, why, she but lost her tongue,
And in a tedious sampler sewed her mind;   40
But, lovely niece, that mean is cut from thee:
A craftier Tereus, cousin, hast thou met,
And he hath cut those pretty fingers off
That could have better sewed than Philomel.
Oh, had the monster seen those lily hands   45
Tremble like aspen leaves upon a lute,
And make the silken strings delight to kiss them,
He would not then have touched them for his life!
Or had he heard the heavenly harmony
Which that sweet tongue hath made,   50
He would have dropped his knife and fell asleep
As Cerberus at the Thracian poet's feet.
Come, let us go and make thy father blind;
For such a sight will blind a father's eye.
One hour's storm will drown the fragrant meads: 55
What will whole months of tears thy father's eyes?
Do not draw back, for we will mourn with thee.
Oh, could our mourning ease thy misery!

Exeunt.

TITUS
ANDRONICUS

ACT III

III. [i.] Titus pleads in vain for his sons' lives, while the judges pass him unheeding. Lucius finally makes him realize that nothing can be done; he himself has been sentenced to perpetual banishment for attempting to rescue his brothers. The spectacle of the mutilated Lavinia, whom Marcus brings before them, causes Titus fresh anguish. Aaron offers a fleeting hope by reporting that if one of the men will send his hand to Saturninus, the latter will send Titus his living sons. After some dispute as to whose hand should be sacrificed, Aaron is happy to grant Titus' request to cut off his. In exchange, Titus is shortly presented with his sons' heads, as Aaron had planned. Titus' passionate grief is replaced by a grim determination to seek revenge for all his wrongs.

<hr>

1. **grave:** mighty.
5. **watched:** remained wakeful.
10. **two-and-twenty sons:** because Titus speaks in I.i. of twenty-one sons who have died honorably, some editors have considered this a discrepancy; but Titus finally allowed Mutius burial in the family vault because of the plea that he had died in an honorable cause, and Mutius could thus be numbered among the twenty-two.

ACT III

[Scene I. Rome. A street.]

Enter the Judges and Senators, with Titus' two sons, bound, passing on the stage to the place of execution, and Titus going before, pleading.

Titus. Hear me, grave fathers! Noble Tribunes, stay!
For pity of mine age, whose youth was spent
In dangerous wars whilst you securely slept;
For all my blood in Rome's great quarrel shed;
For all the frosty nights that I have watched;   5
And for these bitter tears which now you see
Filling the aged wrinkles in my cheeks;
Be pitiful to my condemned sons,
Whose souls is not corrupted as 'tis thought.
For two-and-twenty sons I never wept,   10
Because they died in honor's lofty bed.
*Andronicus lieth down, and the Judges, &c. pass by
                                        him, and Exeunt.*
For these, Tribunes, in the dust I write
My heart's deep languor and my soul's sad tears.
Let my tears stanch the earth's dry appetite;
My sons' sweet blood will make it shame and blush.   15

17. **urns:** pitchers; i.e., tearful eyes.
19. **still:** ever.
22. **So:** provided that.
23. **gentle:** courteous.
36. **bootless:** vainly.
38. **answer:** appease.
39. **in some sort:** in a way.
40. **intercept:** check.
43. **grave weeds:** dignified garments.

O earth, I will befriend thee more with rain,
That shall distill from these two ancient urns,
Than youthful April shall with all his show'rs.
In summer's drought I'll drop upon thee still;
In winter with warm tears I'll melt the snow   20
And keep eternal springtime on thy face,
So thou refuse to drink my dear sons' blood.

Enter Lucius, with his weapon drawn.

O reverend Tribunes! O gentle, aged men!
Unbind my sons, reverse the doom of death;
And let me say, that never wept before,   25
My tears are now prevailing orators.
    Luc. O noble father, you lament in vain.
The Tribunes hear you not: no man is by;
And you recount your sorrows to a stone.
    Titus. Ah, Lucius, for thy brothers let me plead.   30
Grave Tribunes, once more I entreat of you—
    Luc. My gracious lord, no Tribune hears you speak.
    Titus. Why, 'tis no matter, man: if they did hear,
They would not mark me: if they did mark,
They would not pity me; yet plead I must,   35
And bootless unto them.
Therefore I tell my sorrows to the stones,
Who, though they cannot answer my distress,
Yet in some sort they are better than the Tribunes,
For that they will not intercept my tale.   40
When I do weep, they humbly at my feet
Receive my tears and seem to weep with me;
And, were they but attired in grave weeds,

46. offendeth: harmeth.

Aeneas and Anchises leave the burning Troy. From Andrea Alciati, *Emblematum libellus* (1534).

Rome could afford no Tribune like to these.
A stone is soft as wax, Tribunes more hard than stones;   45
A stone is silent and offendeth not,
And Tribunes with their tongues doom men to death.
                                    [*Rises.*]
But wherefore standst thou with thy weapon drawn?
  Luc. To rescue my two brothers from their death:
For which attempt the judges have pronounced   50
My everlasting doom of banishment.
  Titus. O happy man! they have befriended thee.
Why, foolish Lucius, dost thou not perceive
That Rome is but a wilderness of tigers?
Tigers must prey, and Rome affords no prey   55
But me and mine. How happy art thou, then,
From these devourers to be banished!
But who comes with our brother Marcus here?

Enter Marcus with Lavinia.

  Mar. Titus, prepare thy aged eyes to weep;
Or, if not so, thy noble heart to break.   60
I bring consuming sorrow to thine age.
  Titus. Will it consume me? Let me see it then.
  Mar. This was thy daughter.
  Titus.   Why, Marcus, so she is.
  Luc. Ay me, this object kills me!   65
  Titus. Faint-hearted boy, arise, and look upon her.
Speak, Lavinia, what accursed hand
Hath made thee handless in thy father's sight?
What fool hath added water to the sea,
Or brought a fagot to bright-burning Troy?   70

75. **nursed:** nurtured.
77. **effectless:** ineffectual.
83. **engine:** tool.
91. **unrecuring:** incurable.
97. **envious:** hostile.
98. **his:** its; **brinish:** salty.

My grief was at the height before thou camest;
And now, like Nilus, it disdaineth bounds.
Give me a sword; I'll chop off my hands too;
For they have fought for Rome, and all in vain;
And they have nursed this woe in feeding life;   75
In bootless prayer have they been held up,
And they have served me to effectless use.
Now all the service I require of them
Is that the one will help to cut the other.
'Tis well, Lavinia, that thou hast no hands;   80
For hands to do Rome service is but vain.

  Luc. Speak, gentle sister, who hath martyred thee?
  Mar. Oh, that delightful engine of her thoughts,
That blabbed them with such pleasing eloquence,
Is torn from forth that pretty hollow cage,   85
Where, like a sweet melodious bird, it sung
Sweet varied notes, enchanting every ear!
  Luc. Oh, say thou for her, who hath done this deed?
  Mar. Oh, thus I found her straying in the park,
Seeking to hide herself as doth the deer   90
That hath received some unrecuring wound.
  Titus. It was my dear; and he that wounded her
Hath hurt me more than had he killed me dead:
For now I stand as one upon a rock,
Environed with a wilderness of sea,   95
Who marks the waxing tide grow wave by wave,
Expecting ever when some envious surge
Will in his brinish bowels swallow him.
This way to death my wretched sons are gone;
Here stands my other son, a banished man;   100
And here my brother, weeping at my woes.

102. **spurn:** blow.
106. **lively:** living.
110. **this:** this time.
130. **clearness:** purity.

But that which gives my soul the greatest spurn
Is dear Lavinia, dearer than my soul.
Had I but seen thy picture in this plight,
It would have madded me. What shall I do 105
Now I behold thy lively body so?
Thou hast no hands to wipe away thy tears,
Nor tongue to tell me who hath martyred thee.
Thy husband he is dead; and for his death
Thy brothers are condemned, and dead by this. 110
Look, Marcus! ah, son Lucius, look on her!
When I did name her brothers, then fresh tears
Stood on her cheeks, as doth the honey-dew
Upon a gath'red lily almost withered.

   Mar. Perchance she weeps because they killed her 115
     husband;
Perchance because she knows them innocent.

   Titus. If they did kill thy husband, then be joyful,
Because the law hath ta'en revenge on them.
No, no, they would not do so foul a deed; 120
Witness the sorrow that their sister makes.
Gentle Lavinia, let me kiss thy lips;
Or make some sign how I may do thee ease.
Shall thy good uncle and thy brother Lucius
And thou and I sit round about some fountain, 125
Looking all downwards to behold our cheeks
How they are stained, like meadows yet not dry
With miry slime left on them by a flood?
And in the fountain shall we gaze so long,
Till the fresh taste be taken from that clearness 130
And make a brine pit with our bitter tears?
Or shall we cut away our hands like thine?

143. **napkin:** handkerchief.
151. **sympathy:** accord.

Or shall we bite our tongues and in dumb shows
Pass the remainder of our hateful days?
What shall we do? Let us that have our tongues   135
Plot some device of further misery,
To make us wondered at in time to come.

    Luc. Sweet father, cease your tears; for at your grief
See how my wretched sister sobs and weeps.

    Mar. Patience, dear niece. Good Titus, dry thine 140
      eyes.

    Titus. Ah, Marcus, Marcus! brother, well I wot
Thy napkin cannot drink a tear of mine,
For thou, poor man, hast drowned it with thine own.

    Luc. Ah, my Lavinia, I will wipe thy cheeks.   145

    Titus. Mark, Marcus, mark! I understand her signs.
Had she a tongue to speak, now would she say
That to her brother which I said to thee.
His napkin, with his true tears all bewet,
Can do no service on her sorrowful cheeks.   150
Oh, what a sympathy of woe is this,
As far from help as Limbo is from bliss!

Enter Aaron the Moor, alone.

    Aar. Titus Andronicus, my lord the Emperor
Sends thee this word, that, if thou love thy sons,
Let Marcus, Lucius, or thyself, old Titus,   155
Or any one of you, chop off your hand,
And send it to the King. He for the same
Will send thee hither both thy sons alive;
And that shall be the ransom for their fault.

    Titus. O gracious Emperor! O gentle Aaron!   160

184. meet: suitable.

Did ever raven sing so like a lark
That gives sweet tidings of the sun's uprise?
With all my heart I'll send the Emperor
My hand.
Good Aaron, wilt thou help to chop it off?   165
   Luc. Stay, father! for that noble hand of thine,
That hath thrown down so many enemies,
Shall not be sent. My hand will serve the turn.
My youth can better spare my blood than you;
And therefore mine shall save my brothers' lives.   170
   Mar. Which of your hands hath not defended Rome
And reared aloft the bloody battle-ax,
Writing destruction on the enemy's castle?
Oh, none of both but are of high desert.
My hand hath been but idle: let it serve   175
To ransom my two nephews from their death;
Then have I kept it to a worthy end.
   Aar. Nay, come, agree whose hand shall go along,
For fear they die before their pardon come.
   Mar. My hand shall go.   180
   Luc.   By Heaven, it shall not go!
   Titus. Sirs, strive no more. Such withered herbs as
     these
Are meet for plucking up, and therefore mine.
   Luc. Sweet father, if I shall be thought thy son,   185
Let me redeem my brothers both from death.
   Mar. And for our father's sake and mother's care,
Now let me show a brother's love to thee.
   Titus. Agree between you: I will spare my hand.
   Luc. Then I'll go fetch an ax.   190

198–99. **dispatched:** attended to.
201. **warded:** defended.
210. **fat:** delight.

Mar. But I will use the ax.

                Exeunt [Lucius and Marcus].

    Titus. Come hither, Aaron: I'll deceive them both.

Lend me thy hand, and I will give thee mine.

    Aar. [*Aside*] If that be called deceit, I will be honest

And never whilst I live deceive men so.   195

But I'll deceive you in another sort,

And that you'll say ere half an hour pass.

               He cuts off Titus' hand.

       Enter Lucius and Marcus again.

    Titus. Now stay your strife. What shall be is dispatched.

Good Aaron, give His Majesty my hand.   200

Tell him it was a hand that warded him

From thousand dangers: bid him bury it.

More hath it merited: that let it have.

As for my sons, say I account of them

As jewels purchased at an easy price;   205

And yet dear too, because I bought mine own.

    Aar. I go, Andronicus; and for thy hand

Look by and by to have thy sons with thee.

[*Aside*] Their heads, I mean. Oh, how this villainy

Doth fat me with the very thoughts of it!   210

Let fools do good and fair men call for grace,

Aaron will have his soul black like his face.   *Exit.*

    Titus. Oh, here I lift this one hand up to Heaven,

And bow this feeble ruin to the earth.

If any power pities wretched tears,   215

220. **welkin:** skies.
221. **stain:** darken; obscure.
223. **with:** according to.
224. **extremes:** extravagances.
226. **passions:** expressions of passionate grief.
233. **coil:** tumult; disorder.
241. **losers will have leave:** proverbial: "Give losers leave to speak."
242. **stomachs:** bitter resentments.

To that I call! [*To Lavinia*] What, wouldst thou kneel
    with me?
Do, then, dear heart, for Heaven shall hear our
    prayers;
Or with our sighs we'll breathe the welkin dim   220
And stain the sun with fog, as sometime clouds
When they do hug him in their melting bosoms.
   Mar. O brother, speak with possibility,
And do not break into these deep extremes.
   Titus. Is not my sorrow deep, having no bottom?   225
Then be my passions bottomless with them.
   Mar. But yet let reason govern thy lament.
   Titus. If there were reason for these miseries,
Then into limits could I bind my woes.
When heaven doth weep, doth not the earth o'erflow? 230
If the winds rage, doth not the sea wax mad,
Threat'ning the welkin with his big-swoln face?
And wilt thou have a reason for this coil?
I am the sea: hark, how her sighs doth blow!
She is the weeping welkin, I the earth.   235
Then must my sea be moved with her sighs;
Then must my earth with her continual tears
Become a deluge, overflowed and drowned.
Forwhy my bowels cannot hide her woes,
But like a drunkard must I vomit them.   240
Then give me leave, for losers will have leave
To ease their stomachs with their bitter tongues.

    Enter a Messenger, with two heads and a hand.

   Mess. Worthy Andronicus, ill art thou repaid

247. **sports:** amusement.

253. **some deal:** a bit.

254. **flouted at:** mocked.

257. **shrink:** give way; collapse.

258. **death should let life bear his name:** i.e., what is really death should be allowed to call itself life.

259. **interest:** legal title; right; **to breathe:** breathing; i.e., only the fact that Titus breathes entitles his state to be called life.

260. **comfortless:** nonrestorative; ineffectual.

263. **flatt'ry:** pleasing delusion.

266. **dear:** dire.

For that good hand thou sentst the Emperor.
Here are the heads of thy two noble sons;   245
And here's thy hand, in scorn to thee sent back:
Thy grief their sports, thy resolution mocked;
That woe is me to think upon thy woes,
More than remembrance of my father's death.   *Exit.*

  Mar. Now let hot Etna cool in Sicily,   250
And be my heart an ever-burning hell!
These miseries are more than may be borne.
To weep with them that weep doth ease some deal,
But sorrow flouted at is double death.

  Luc. Ah, that this sight should make so deep a   255
    wound
And yet detested life not shrink thereat!
That ever death should let life bear his name,
Where life hath no more interest but to breathe!
                   [Lavinia kisses Titus.]

  Mar. Alas, poor heart, that kiss is comfortless   260
As frozen water to a starved snake.

  Titus. When will this fearful slumber have an end?

  Mar. Now, farewell, flatt'ry: die, Andronicus!
Thou dost not slumber. See, thy two sons' heads,
Thy warlike hand, thy mangled daughter here,   265
Thy other banished son with this dear sight
Struck pale and bloodless, and thy brother, I,
Even like a stony image, cold and numb.
Ah, now no more will I control thy griefs!
Rent off thy silver hair, thy other hand   270
Gnawing with thy teeth, and be this dismal sight
The closing-up of our most wretched eyes.
Now is a time to storm. Why art thou still?

278. **usurp upon:** exert a tyrant's power over.
279. **tributary:** i.e., exacted as tribute.
283. **mischiefs:** injuries; **returned:** repaid.
286. **heavy:** sorrowful.
301. **pledges:** hostages.
303. **tofore:** heretofore.

The defeat of Tarquinius Superbus. From Livy, *Historicus duobus libri auctos* (1520). (See l. 308.)

Titus. Ha, ha, ha!

 Mar. Why dost thou laugh? It fits not with this hour. 275

 Titus. Why, I have not another tear to shed.

Besides, this sorrow is an enemy

And would usurp upon my wat'ry eyes

And make them blind with tributary tears.

Then which way shall I find Revenge's cave? 280

For these two heads do seem to speak to me

And threat me I shall never come to bliss

Till all these mischiefs be returned again

Even in their throats that hath committed them.

Come, let me see what task I have to do. 285

You heavy people, circle me about,

That I may turn me to each one of you

And swear unto my soul to right your wrongs.

The vow is made. Come, brother, take a head;

And in this hand the other will I bear. 290

And Lavinia, thou shalt be employed:

Bear thou my hand, sweet wench, between thy teeth.

As for thee, boy, go get thee from my sight:

Thou art an exile, and thou must not stay.

Hie to the Goths and raise an army there. 295

And, if ye love me, as I think you do,

Let's kiss and part, for we have much to do.

       Exeunt. Manet Lucius.

 Luc. Farewell, Andronicus, my noble father,

The woeful'st man that ever lived in Rome.

Farewell, proud Rome: till Lucius come again, 300

He leaves his pledges dearer than his life.

Farewell, Lavinia, my noble sister:

Oh, would thou wert as thou tofore hast been!

304. **nor . . . nor:** neither . . . nor.

305. **But in oblivion and hateful griefs:** i.e.,
what they once were is lost in oblivion, and they
exist only as embodiments of hate-provoking grievances, personifications of revenge.

307. **proud:** cruel.

308. **Tarquin:** Tarquinius Superbus, last King of
Rome, who was expelled after his son, Sextus, raped
Lucrece.

309. **pow'r:** army.

▬▬▬▬▬▬▬▬▬▬▬▬▬▬▬▬

III. [ii.] The grief-stricken Titus shares a frugal
meal with Marcus, Lavinia, and his grandson, Lucius.
Marcus momentarily cheers Titus by killing a fly,
because, he says, it resembleed the Moor. Titus'
triumph at this mock killing of Aaron causes Marcus
to fear for his sanity.

▬▬▬▬▬▬▬▬▬▬▬▬

4. **sorrow-wreathen knot:** i.e., his folded arms,
that express his melancholy.

6. **passionate:** express with passionate action.

8. **tyrannize:** do violence.

But now nor Lucius nor Lavinia lives
But in oblivion and hateful griefs. 305
If Lucius live, he will requite your wrongs
And make proud Saturnine and his Empress
Beg at the gates, like Tarquin and his queen.
Now will I to the Goths and raise a pow'r,
To be revenged on Rome and Saturnine. 310

Exit.

[Scene II. A room in Titus' house. A banquet set out.]

*Enter Titus Andronicus, Marcus, Lavinia, and the Boy
Lucius.*

Titus. So, so, now sit: and look you eat no more
Than will preserve just so much strength in us
As will revenge these bitter woes of ours.
Marcus, unknit that sorrow-wreathen knot.
Thy niece and I, poor creatures, want our hands 5
And cannot passionate our tenfold grief
With folded arms. This poor right hand of mine
Is left to tyrannize upon my breast;
Who, when my heart, all mad with misery,
Beats in this hollow prison of my flesh, 10
Then thus I thump it down.
[*To Lavinia*] Thou map of woe, that thus dost talk in
signs!
When thy poor heart beats with outrageous beating,
Thou canst not strike it thus to make it still. 15

21. **fool:** an epithet of affectionate compassion rather than contempt.

23. **tender:** youthful.

24. **dote:** become foolish.

28. **urge:** mention.

33. **square:** frame.

40. **meshed:** variant of "mashed," brewed.

42. **perfect:** perfectly informed.

45. **wink:** close the eyes.

Wound it with sighing, girl, kill it with groans;
Or get some little knife between thy teeth
And just against thy heart make thou a hole,
That all the tears that thy poor eyes let fall
May run into that sink and, soaking in,   20
Drown the lamenting fool in sea-salt tears.

Mar. Fie, brother, fie! teach her not thus to lay
Such violent hands upon her tender life.

Titus. How now! has sorrow made thee dote al-
        ready?   25
Why, Marcus, no man should be mad but I.
What violent hands can she lay on her life?
Ah, wherefore dost thou urge the name of hands,
To bid Aeneas tell the tale twice o'er
How Troy was burnt and he made miserable?   30
Oh, handle not the theme, to talk of hands,
Lest we remember still that we have none.
Fie, fie, how franticly I square my talk,
As if we should forget we had no hands
If Marcus did not name the word of hands!   35
Come, let's fall to; and, gentle girl, eat this.
Here is no drink. Hark, Marcus, what she says.
I can interpret all her martyred signs:
She says she drinks no other drink but tears,
Brewed with her sorrow, meshed upon her cheeks.   40
Speechless complainer, I will learn thy thought;
In thy dumb action will I be as perfect
As begging hermits in their holy prayers.
Thou shalt not sigh, nor hold thy stumps to Heaven,
Nor wink, nor nod, nor kneel, nor make a sign,   45
But I of these will wrest an alphabet

47. **still:** continual.
50. **merry:** cheerful.
51. **passion:** grief.
71. **ill-favored:** ugly.
76. **insult on:** exult over.

And by still practice learn to know thy meaning.

  Boy. Good grandsire, leave these bitter deep laments.

Make my aunt merry with some pleasing tale.   50

  Mar. Alas, the tender boy, in passion moved,

Doth weep to see his grandsire's heaviness.

  Titus. Peace, tender sapling! Thou art made of tears,

And tears will quickly melt thy life away.

                Marcus strikes the dish with a knife.

What dost thou strike at, Marcus, with thy knife?   55

  Mar. At that that I have killed, my lord—a fly.

  Titus. Out on thee, murderer! Thou killst my heart.

Mine eyes are cloyed with view of tyranny.

A deed of death done on the innocent

Becomes not Titus' brother. Get thee gone: 60

I see thou art not for my company.

  Mar. Alas, my lord, I have but killed a fly.

  Titus. "But!" How if that fly had a father and mother?

How would he hang his slender gilded wings   65

And buzz lamenting doings in the air!

Poor harmless fly,

That with his pretty buzzing melody

Came here to make us merry! And thou hast killed him.   70

  Mar. Pardon me, sir: it was a black, ill-favored fly,

Like to the Empress' Moor. Therefore I killed him.

  Titus. Oh, oh, oh!

Then pardon me for reprehending thee,

For thou hast done a charitable deed.   75

Give me thy knife, I will insult on him,

77. **Flattering:** deceiving pleasantly.
87. **closet:** chamber.
90. **dazzle:** blur.

Flattering myself as if it were the Moor
Come hither purposely to poison me.
There's for thyself, and that's for Tamora.
Ah, sirrah!   80
Yet, I think, we are not brought so low
But that between us we can kill a fly
That comes in likeness of a coal-black Moor.
  Mar. Alas, poor man! grief has so wrought on him,
He takes false shadows for true substances.   85
  Titus. Come, take away. Lavinia, go with me.
I'll to thy closet and go read with thee
Sad stories chanced in the times of old.
Come, boy, and go with me. Thy sight is young,
And thou shalt read when mine begin to dazzle.   90

                                        Exeunt.

TITUS
ANDRONICUS

ACT IV

IV. [i.] Young Lucius is frightened at the way in which Lavinia follows him about. Her object is revealed when she turns the pages of the boy's copy of Ovid's *Metamorphoses* to the tale of Philomela's rape by Tereus. Aided by Titus, Lavinia uses her arm stumps to write the names of her ravishers in the dirt. Titus has them all kneel and swear vengeance upon their enemies: Tamora and her sons.

▬▬▬▬▬▬▬▬▬▬▬▬▬

13. **Cornelia:** mother of the Roman tribunes Tiberius and Gaius Gracchus, whom she called her "jewels."

15. **Tully's Orator:** the *De oratore* of Marcus Tullius Cicero.

16. **plies:** solicits.

ACT IV

[Scene I.   Rome.   Titus' garden.]

Enter Lucius' Son and Lavinia running after him, and the Boy flies her, with his books under his arm. Enter Titus and Marcus.

Boy. Help, grandsire, help! My aunt Lavinia
Follows me everywhere, I know not why.
Good uncle Marcus, see how swift she comes.
Alas, sweet aunt, I know not what you mean.
   Mar. Stand by me, Lucius. Do not fear thine aunt.   5
   Titus. She loves thee, boy, too well to do thee harm.
   Boy. Ay, when my father was in Rome she did.
   Mar. What means my niece Lavinia by these signs?
   Titus. Fear her not, Lucius. Somewhat doth she
     mean.   10
See, Lucius, see how much she makes of thee.
Somewhither would she have thee go with her.
Ah, boy, Cornelia never with more care
Read to her sons than she hath read to thee
Sweet poetry and Tully's *Orator*.   15
Canst thou not guess wherefore she plies thee thus?
   Boy. My lord, I know not, I, nor can I guess,

57

25. **fury:** madness.
34. **skilled:** educated.
36. **beguile:** divert.
38. **in sequence:** one after the other.
41. **fact:** crime.

Unless some fit or frenzy do possess her.
For I have heard my grandsire say full oft,
Extremity of griefs would make men mad; 20
And I have read that Hecuba of Troy
Ran mad for sorrow. That made me to fear;
Although, my lord, I know my noble aunt
Loves me as dear as e'er my mother did,
And would not, but in fury, fright my youth: 2£
Which made me down to throw my books and fly,
Causeless perhaps. But pardon me, sweet aunt.
And, madam, if my uncle Marcus go,
I will most willingly attend your Ladyship.
   Mar. Lucius, I will. 30
[*Lavinia turns over with her stumps the books which
               Lucius has let fall.*]
   Titus. How now, Lavinia! Marcus, what means this?
Some book there is that she desires to see.
Which is it, girl, of these? Open them, boy.
But thou art deeper read and better skilled.
Come, and take choice of all my library, 35
And so beguile thy sorrow till the Heavens
Reveal the damned contriver of this deed.
Why lifts she up her arms in sequence thus?
   Mar. I think she means that there were more than
     one 40
Confederate in the fact. Ay, more there was;
Or else to Heaven she heaves them for revenge.
   Titus. Lucius, what book is that she tosseth so?
   Boy. Grandsire, 'tis Ovid's *Metamorphoses*.
My mother gave it me. 45
   Mar.   For love of her that's gone,

47. **culled:** selected.

53. **root of thy annoy:** the reason for thy mutilation.

54. **quotes:** takes note of.

62. **Patterned by:** patterned after; resembling.

The Fates decree, that 'tis a mighty wrong;
To Woemen Kinde, to have more Greif, then Tongue

Lucrece about to stab herself. Frontispiece to Shakespeare's
Rape of Lucrece (1655).

Perhaps she culled it from among the rest.

   Titus. Soft! so busily she turns the leaves!
Help her.
What would she find? Lavinia, shall I read?   50
This is the tragic tale of Philomel,
And treats of Tereus' treason and his rape;
And rape, I fear, was root of thy annoy.

   Mar. See, brother, see! Note how she quotes the
     leaves.   55

   Titus. Lavinia, wert thou thus surprised, sweet girl,
Ravished and wronged, as Philomela was,
Forced in the ruthless, vast, and gloomy woods?
See, see!
Ay, such a place there is where we did hunt—   60
Oh, had we never, never hunted there!—
Patterned by that the poet here describes,
By nature made for murders and for rapes.

   Mar. Oh, why should nature build so foul a den,
Unless the gods delight in tragedies?   65

   Titus. Give signs, sweet girl, for here are none but
     friends,
What Roman lord it was durst do the deed:
Or slunk not Saturnine, as Tarquin erst,
That left the camp to sin in Lucrece' bed?   70

   Mar. Sit down, sweet niece. Brother, sit down by
     me.
Apollo, Pallas, Jove, or Mercury,
Inspire me, that I may this treason find!
My lord, look here. Look here, Lavinia.   75
He writes his name with his staff, and guides it with
feet and mouth.

79. **shift:** device.

85. **Stuprum:** rape.

88–9. **Magni . . . vides:** "Great ruler of the heavens, are you so slow to hear of crimes and to observe them?" (slightly altered from Seneca, *Phaedra* 671–2).

93. **exclaims:** loud outcries.

95. **Roman Hector's hope:** i.e., the promising son of the man who is Rome's greatest warrior, as Hector was of Troy.

96. **fere:** husband.

98. **Junius Brutus:** nephew of Tarquinius Superbus, who led the revolt against him in outrage at his son's crime.

99. **by good advice:** after careful planning.

101. **with this reproach:** of this disgrace.

102. **and:** if.

104. **wind:** get wind of.

This sandy plot is plain. Guide, if thou canst,
This after me. I have writ my name
Without the help of any hand at all.
Cursed be that heart that forced us to this shift!
Write thou, good niece, and here display at last   80
What God will have discovered for revenge.
Heaven guide thy pen to print thy sorrows plain,
That we may know the traitors and the truth!

She takes the staff in her mouth, and guides it with
her stumps, and writes.

    Titus. Oh, do ye read, my lord, what she hath writ?
Stuprum. Chiron. Demetrius.   85
    Mar. What, what! the lustful sons of Tamora
Performers of this heinous, bloody deed?
    Titus. Magni Dominator poli,
Tam lentus audis scelera? tam lentus vides?
    Mar. Oh, calm thee, gentle lord: although I know   90
There is enough written upon this earth
To stir a mutiny in the mildest thoughts
And arm the minds of infants to exclaims.
My lord, kneel down with me; Lavinia, kneel;
And kneel, sweet boy, the Roman Hector's hope;   95
And swear with me, as, with the woeful fere
And father of that chaste dishonored dame,
Lord Junius Brutus sware for Lucrece' rape,
That we will prosecute by good advice
Mortal revenge upon these traitorous Goths   100
And see their blood, or die with this reproach.
    Titus. 'Tis sure enough, and you knew how.
But if you hunt these bear whelps, then beware.
The dam will wake; and, if she wind ye once,

107. **list:** please.

108. **let alone:** don't meddle with the affair.

109. **a leaf of brass:** reflecting a proverbial saying to the effect that the memory of wrongs is relentlessly nursed; see cut.

112. **Sibyl's leaves:** in the *Aeneid*, bk. vi, the Cumaean Sibyl writes her prophecies on leaves, so that Aeneas fears that the one meant for him will blow away in the wind.

121. **fit:** outfit.

124. **message:** errand.

128. **brave it:** swagger.

129. **marry:** indeed; **waited on:** attended; heeded.

132. **ecstasy:** madness.

"In marble hard our harms we always grave,
    Because we still will bear the same in mind."
An emblematic representation of a proverbial idea.
From Geoffrey Whitney, *A Choice of Emblems* (1586).

She's with the lion deeply still in league　　　　　　105
And lulls him whilst she playeth on her back,
And when he sleeps will she do what she list.
You are a young huntsman, Marcus: let alone;
And, come, I will go get a leaf of brass
And with a gad of steel will write these words　　　110
And lay it by. The angry northern wind
Will blow these sands, like Sibyl's leaves, abroad,
And where's our lesson then? Boy, what say you?

　　Boy. I say, my lord, that if I were a man,
Their mother's bedchamber should not be safe　　115
For these base bondmen to the yoke of Rome.

　　Mar. Ay, that's my boy! Thy father hath full oft
For his ungrateful country done the like.

　　Boy. And, uncle, so will I, and if I live.

　　Titus. Come, go with me into mine armory.　　120
Lucius, I'll fit thee, and withal, my boy
Shall carry from me to the Empress' sons
Presents that I intend to send them both.
Come, come: thou'lt do my message, wilt thou not?

　　Boy. Ay, with my dagger in their bosoms, grandsire. 125

　　Titus. No, boy, not so: I'll teach thee another course.
Lavinia, come. Marcus, look to my house.
Lucius and I'll go brave it at the court:
Ay, marry, will we, sir; and we'll be waited on.
　　　　　　Exeunt [*Titus, Lavinia, and young Lucius*].

　　Mar. O Heavens, can you hear a good man groan　130
And not relent, or not compassion him?
Marcus, attend him in his ecstasy,
That hath more scars of sorrow in his heart
Than foemen's marks upon his battered shield,

136. **Revenge the Heavens:** may the Heavens revenge.

▬▬▬▬▬▬▬▬▬▬▬▬▬▬▬▬▬▬▬▬▬▬▬

IV. [ii.] Young Lucius bears a threatening message to Demetrius and Chiron, veiled in a quotation from Horace's *Odes*. Only Aaron realizes that the message reveals Titus' knowledge of their guilt. A nurse enters with a black child, which Tamora has borne. Aaron is delighted with what is obviously his offspring, but Tamora's sons feel the disgrace will be their mother's ruin and threaten to kill the infant. Aaron holds them off with his sword and reveals a plan to substitute another Moorish child of light complexion, whose parents will be pleased to bring up Aaron's baby in order to give their own child a place in the imperial family. He kills the nurse and orders Demetrius and Chiron to dispose of the body while he visits his Moorish friends to arrange for his child's care.

▬▬▬▬▬▬▬▬▬▬▬▬▬▬▬▬▬

7. **confound:** destroy.
10. **deciphered:** revealed.
13. **well advised:** thoughtfully; not insanely.
15. **gratify:** please.

But yet so just that he will not revenge.   135
Revenge the Heavens for old Andronicus!

                                        Exit.

░░

[Scene II.   Rome.   A room in the palace.]

*Enter Aaron, Chiron, and Demetrius at one door; and
at the other door young Lucius and another, with a
bundle of weapons and verses writ upon them.*

  Chir. Demetrius, here's the son of Lucius:
He hath some message to deliver us.
  Aar. Ay, some mad message from his mad grand-
father.
  Boy. My lords, with all the humbleness I may,   5
I greet your Honors from Andronicus.
[*Aside*] And pray the Roman gods confound you
both!
  Dem. Gramercy, lovely Lucius. What's the news?
  Boy. [*Aside*] That you are both deciphered, that's   10
the news,
For villains marked with rape.—May it please you,
My grandsire, well advised, hath sent by me
The goodliest weapons of his armory
To gratify your honorable youth,   15
The hope of Rome; for so he bid me say:
And so I do, and with his gifts present
Your Lordships that, whenever you have need,
You may be armed and appointed well.

24–5. **Integer . . . arcu:** "The man who is upright in life and unstained by crime has no need of Moorish darts" (Horace, *Odes* I.xxii.1–2).

27. **the grammar:** the Latin grammar of William Lily, which was widely used in Elizabethan grammar schools.

28. **just:** exactly.

30. **no sound jest:** ironical, meaning the reverse.

34. **witty:** intelligent; **well afoot:** i.e., not confined to bed.

35. **conceit:** clever idea.

36. **unrest:** i.e., the labor of childbirth.

37. **happy:** fortunate.

43. **insinuate:** try to please.

47. **At such a bay:** so at our mercy (like a cornered animal).

And so I leave you both, [*Aside*] like bloody villains. 20
       Exeunt [*Boy and Attendant*].
 Dem. What's here? A scroll, and written round
  about!
Let's see:

  Integer vitae, scelerisque purus,
  Non eget Mauri jaculis, nec arcu.   25

 Chir. Oh, 'tis a verse in Horace; I know it well.
I read it in the grammar long ago.
 Aar. Ay, just, a verse in Horace: right, you have it.
[*Aside*] Now, what a thing it is to be an ass!
Here's no sound jest: the old man hath found their 30
 guilt,
And sends them weapons wrapped about with lines
That wound, beyond their feeling, to the quick.
But were our witty Empress well afoot,
She would applaud Andronicus' conceit.   35
But let her rest in her unrest awhile.—
And now, young lords, was't not a happy star
Led us to Rome, strangers, and more than so,
Captives, to be advanced to this height?
It did me good, before the palace gate   40
To brave the Tribune in his brother's hearing.
 Dem. But me more good to see so great a lord
Basely insinuate and send us gifts.
 Aar. Had he not reason, Lord Demetrius?
Did you not use his daughter very friendly?   45
 Dem. I would we had a thousand Roman dames
At such a bay, by turn to serve our lust.

48. **charitable:** punning on the sense of "charity" connoting Christian love.

55. **over:** up.

57. **Belike:** very likely.

61. **whit:** probably a poor pun on "white."

Chir. A charitable wish and full of love.

Aar. Here lacks but your mother for to say Amen.

Chir. And that would she for twenty thousand   50
more.

Dem. Come, let us go and pray to all the gods
For our beloved mother in her pains.

Aar. [*Aside*] Pray to the devils: the gods have
given us over.   *Trumpets sound.*   55

Dem. Why do the Emperor's trumpets flourish thus?

Chir. Belike, for joy the Emperor hath a son.

Dem. Soft! who comes here?

Enter Nurse, with a blackamoor Child.

Nurse.   Good morrow, lords.
Oh, tell me, did you see Aaron the Moor?   60

Aar. Well, more or less, or ne'er a whit at all.
Here Aaron is: and what with Aaron now?

Nurse. O gentle Aaron, we are all undone!
Now help, or woe betide thee evermore!

Aar. Why, what a caterwauling dost thou keep!   65
What dost thou wrap and fumble in thy arms?

Nurse. Oh, that which I would hide from Heaven's
eye,
Our Empress' shame and stately Rome's disgrace!
She is delivered lords, she is delivered.   70

Aar. To whom?

Nurse.   I mean, she is brought abed.

Aar. Well, God give her good rest! What hath he
sent her?

Nurse. A devil.   75

77. **issue:** (1) offspring; (2) outcome.

83. **Zounds:** God's wounds.

84. **blowze:** "a fat, red-faced wench" (*New English Dictionary*). Aaron is sardonic. The word also suggests the dialectal word "bloss" (etymologically connected with "blossom") that was used ironically of "any ugly sight; a 'fright'" (*English Dialect Dictionary*).

88. **done:** used sexually.

98. **broach:** spit.

103. **got:** begot.

Aar.   Why, then she is the Devil's dam:
A joyful issue.

Nurse. A joyless, dismal, black, and sorrowful issue.
Here is the babe, as loathsome as a toad
Amongst the fairfaced breeders of our clime.   80
The Empress sends it thee, thy stamp, thy seal,
And bids thee christen it with thy dagger's point.

Aar. Zounds, ye whore! is black so base a hue?
Sweet blowze, you are a beauteous blossom, sure.

Dem. Villain, what hast thou done?   85

Aar. That which thou canst not undo.

Chir. Thou hast undone our mother.

Aar. Villain, I have done thy mother.

Dem. And therein, hellish dog, thou hast undone
    her.   90
Woe to her chance and damned her loathed choice!
Accursed the offspring of so foul a fiend!

Chir. It shall not live.

Aar. It shall not die.

Nurse. Aaron, it must: the mother wills it so.   95

Aar. What, must it, nurse? Then let no man but I
Do execution on my flesh and blood.

Dem. I'll broach the tadpole on my rapier's point.
Nurse, give it me: my sword shall soon dispatch it.

Aar. Sooner this sword shall plow thy bowels up.   100
     [*Takes the Child from the Nurse, and draws.*]
Stay, murderous villains! Will you kill your brother?
Now, by the burning tapers of the sky
That shone so brightly when this boy was got,
He dies upon my scimitar's sharp point
That touches this my first-born son and heir!   105

106. **Enceladus:** one of the hundred-armed giants who fought with the gods in Greek mythology.

107. **Typhon:** a monstrous serpent that disgorged flaming rocks from his mouth, associated with the volcanic action of Mt. Etna, under which he was finally buried after his defeat by Zeus. His offspring included Cerberus and the Lernean Hydra.

108. **Alcides:** the grandson of Alcaeus; i.e., Hercules, who subdued both Cerberus and the Hydra.

110. **sanguine:** referring to the **sanguine** temperament, which was characterized by a ruddy complexion, courage, and an optimistic and amorous disposition. Their blooming complexions belie their **shallow-hearted** (cowardly) natures, in Aaron's opinion.

111. **white-limed walls:** i.e., "whited sepulchers" (Matt. 23:27); hypocrites.

113. **it scorns to bear another hue:** proverbially, "Black will take no other hue."

118 **excuse:** explain.

121. **The vigor and the picture:** the vigorous image.

124. **smoke:** suffer severely; smart.

126. **foul:** wicked; **escape:** escapade.

129. **ignomy:** ignominy; infamy.

130. **your beauty bears:** i.e., that their fair complexions carry with them.

132. **close enacts:** secret acts.

133. **leer:** facial hue.

136. **sensibly fed:** nourished so that he has life and feeling.

I tell you, younglings, not Enceladus,
With all his threat'ning band of Typhon's brood,
Nor great Alcides, nor the god of war,
Shall seize this prey out of his father's hands.
What, what, ye sanguine, shallow-hearted boys! 110
Ye white-limed walls! ye alehouse painted signs!
Coal-black is better than another hue
In that it scorns to bear another hue;
For all the water in the ocean
Can never turn the swan's black legs to white, 115
Although she lave them hourly in the flood.
Tell the Empress from me I am of age
To keep mine own, excuse it how she can.
　　Dem. Wilt thou betray thy noble mistress thus?
　　Aar. My mistress is my mistress, this myself, 120
The vigor and the picture of my youth.
This before all the world do I prefer;
This mauger all the world will I keep safe,
Or some of you shall smoke for it in Rome.
　　Dem. By this our mother is forever shamed. 125
　　Chir. Rome will despise her for this foul escape.
　　Nurse. The Emperor in his rage will doom her
　　　　death.
　　Chir. I blush to think upon this ignomy.
　　Aar. Why, there's the privilege your beauty bears. 130
Fie, treacherous hue, that will betray with blushing
The close enacts and counsels of thy heart!
Here's a young lad framed of another leer.
Look how the black slave smiles upon the father,
As who should say, "Old lad, I am thine own." 135
He is your brother, lords, sensibly fed

137. **self:** same.

140. **by the surer side:** proverbial: "The mother's side is the surer side."

143. **Advise thee:** bethink yourself; consider carefully.

144. **subscribe:** agree.

145. **so:** provided that.

147. **have the wind of you:** stay on the safe side of you.

150. **brave:** excellent; fine.

158. **Two may keep counsel when the third's away:** proverbial.

164. **policy:** shrewdness.

Pluto, the god who ruled the underworld, using Cerberus as a footrest. From Georg Pictorius, *Apothesos tam exterarum gentium quam Romanorum deorum* (1558). (See l. 107, note.)

Of that self blood that first gave life to you;
And from that womb where you imprisoned were
He is enfranchised and come to light.
Nay, he is your brother by the surer side,   140
Although my seal be stamped in his face.

   Nurse. Aaron, what shall I say unto the Empress?

   Dem. Advise thee, Aaron, what is to be done,
And we will all subscribe to thy advice.
Save thou the child, so we may all be safe.   145

   Aar. Then sit we down and let us all consult.
My son and I will have the wind of you.
Keep there: now talk at pleasure of your safety.

                                [They sit.]

   Dem. How many women saw this child of his?

   Aar. Why, so, brave lords! When we join in league, 150
I am a lamb: but if you brave the Moor,
The chafed boar, the mountain lioness,
The ocean swells not so as Aaron storms.
But say, again, how many saw the child?

   Nurse. Cornelia the midwife and myself;   155
And no one else but the delivered Empress.

   Aar. The Empress, the midwife, and yourself.
Two may keep counsel when the third's away.
Go to the Empress, tell her this I said.   *He kills her.*
Weke, weke!   160
So cries a pig prepared to the spit.

   Dem. What meanst thou, Aaron? Wherefore didst
     thou this?

   Aar. O Lord, sir, 'tis a deed of policy.
Shall she live to betray this guilt of ours,   165
A long-tongued babbling gossip? No, lords, no.

171. **pack:** conspire.
172. **circumstance:** details.
178. **physic:** medicine.
179. **bestow:** take care of.
180. **gallant grooms:** splendid fellows.
182. **presently:** immediately.
193. **puts us to our shifts:** forces us to contrive.

And now be it known to you my full intent.
Not far one Muli lives, my countryman,
His wife but yesternight was brought to bed;
His child is like to her, fair as you are.   170
Go pack with him and give the mother gold,
And tell them both the circumstance of all,
And how by this their child shall be advanced,
And be received for the Emperor's heir
And substituted in the place of mine,   175
To calm this tempest whirling in the court:
And let the Emperor dandle him for his own.
Hark ye, lords: you see I have given her physic,

> *[Pointing to the Nurse.]*

And you must needs bestow her funeral.
The fields are near, and you are gallant grooms.   180
This done, see that you take no longer days
But send the midwife presently to me.
The midwife and the nurse well made away,
Then let the ladies tattle what they please.

   Chir. Aaron, I see thou wilt not trust the air   185
With secrets.

   Dem.   For this care of Tamora,
Herself and hers are highly bound to thee.

Exeunt [Demetrius and Chiron bearing off the Nurse's
body.]

   Aar. Now to the Goths, as swift as swallow flies;
There to dispose this treasure in mine arms   190
And secretly to greet the Empress' friends.
Come on, you thick-lipped slave, I'll bear you hence;
For it is you that puts us to our shifts.
I'll make you feed on berries and on roots,

IV. [**iii.**] Titus amuses himself by shooting arrows in public places, bearing messages to the gods. A rustic, on his way to seek a favor at the imperial court, is entrusted with a so-called "supplication" to Saturninus, in the folds of which a knife is concealed.

████████████████████

4. **home:** fully.

5. **Terras Astraea reliquit:** "Justice has left the earth." Astraea, goddess of justice, fled to Heaven in horror at man's wickedness during the Iron Age and became the constellation Virgo (Ovid, *Metamorphoses*, bk. i).

6. **remembered:** reminded.

9. **Happily:** perhaps.

The constellation Virgo, metamorphosis of Astraea, goddess of justice. From Hyginus, *Fabularum liber* (1535).

And feed on curds and whey, and suck the goat,   195
And cabin in a cave, and bring you up
To be a warrior and command a camp.

Exit.

Scene III.   [Rome.   A public place.]

Enter Titus, old Marcus, Young Lucius, and other
Gentlemen [Publius, Sempronius, and Caius], with
bows; and Titus bears the arrows with letters on the
ends of them.

   Titus. Come, Marcus, come: kinsmen, this is the
        way.
Sir boy, let me see your archery:
Look ye draw home enough, and 'tis there straight.
Terras Astraea reliquit: 5
Be you remembered, Marcus, she's gone, she's fled.
Sirs, take you to your tools. You, cousins, shall
Go sound the ocean and cast your nets:
Happily you may catch her in the sea.
Yet there's as little justice as at land.   10
No! Publius and Sempronius, you must do it:
'Tis you must dig with mattock and with spade,
And pierce the inmost center of the earth.
Then, when you come to Pluto's region,
I pray you, deliver him this petition: 15
Tell him, it is for justice and for aid,
And that it comes from old Andronicus,
Shaken with sorrows in ungrateful Rome.

20. **What time:** at which time.

25. **pipe:** whistle.

31. **careful:** thoughtful, hence likely to be effective.

34. **reak:** vengeance.

44. **burning lake:** probably the fiery river Phlegethon in Hades.

Cyclopes. From Ovid, *Metamorphoses* (1509).

Ah, Rome! Well, well, I made thee miserable
What time I threw the people's suffrages   20
On him that thus doth tyrannize o'er me.
Go, get you gone; and pray be careful all,
And leave you not a man-of-war unsearched.
This wicked Emperor may have shipped her hence;
And, kinsmen, then we may go pipe for justice.   25
 Mar. O Publius, is not this a heavy case,
To see thy noble uncle thus distract?
 Pub. Therefore, my lord, it highly us concerns
By day and night t' attend him carefully
And feed his humor kindly as we may   30
Till time beget some careful remedy.
 Mar. Kinsmen, his sorrows are past remedy.
Join with the Goths and with revengeful war
Take wreak on Rome for this ingratitude,
And vengeance on the traitor Saturnine.   35
 Titus. Publius, how now! How now, my masters!
What, have you met with her?
 Pub. No, my good lord, but Pluto sends you word,
If you will have Revenge from hell, you shall.
Marry, for Justice, she is so employed,   40
He thinks, with Jove in Heaven, or somewhere else,
So that perforce you must needs stay a time.
 Titus. He doth me wrong to feed me with delays.
I'll dive into the burning lake below
And pull her out of Acheron by the heels.   45
Marcus, we are but shrubs, no cedars we,
No big-boned men framed of the Cyclops' size;
But metal, Marcus, steel to the very back,
Yet wrung with wrongs more than our backs can bear.

53. **gear:** business.
56. **Pallas:** Athena.
58. **good:** successful.
64–5. **well said:** well done.
68. **Jubiter:** an old form of the name, probably used to make possible the Clown's mistake in line 80.
76. **villain:** servant, but punning on the other sense, referring to Aaron.
77. **should not choose:** could not help.

And sith there's no justice in earth nor hell,   50
We will solicit Heaven and move the gods
To send down Justice for to wreak our wrongs.
Come, to this gear. You are a good archer, Marcus;
                              He gives them the arrows.
Ad Jovem, that's for you. Here, *Ad Apollinem.*
Ad Martem, that's for myself.   55
Here, boy, to Pallas. Here, to Mercury.
To Saturn, Caius, not to Saturnine!
You were as good to shoot against the wind.
To it, boy! Marcus, loose when I bid.
Of my word, I have written to effect: 60
There's not a god left unsolicited.
  Mar. Kinsmen, shoot all your shafts into the court.
We will afflict the Emperor in his pride.
  Titus. Now, masters, draw. [*They shoot*] Oh, well
    said, Lucius!   65
Good boy, in Virgo's lap! Give it Pallas.
  Mar. My lord, I aim a mile beyond the moon:
Your letter is with Jubiter by this.
  Titus. Ha, ha!
Publius, Publius, what hast thou done?   70
See, see, thou hast shot off one of Taurus' horns.
  Mar. This was the sport, my lord. When Publius
    shot,
The Bull, being galled, gave Aries such a knock
That down fell both the Ram's horns in the court;   75
And who should find them but the Empress' villain?
She laughed and told the Moor he should not choose
But give them to his master for a present.

84. gibbet maker: the Clown misunderstands **Jubiter** (Jupiter), which he interprets as "gibbeter."

96. tribunal plebs: tribunes of the people; **take up:** settle.

97. Emperal's: Emperor's, a typical clown's mistake.

102. with a grace: gracefully.

Titus. Why, there it goes: God give His Lordship joy! 80

Enter the Clown, with a basket, and two pigeons in it.

News, news from Heaven! Marcus, the post is come.
Sirrah, what tidings? Have you any letters?
Shall I have justice? What says Jubiter?

Clown. Ho, the gibbet maker! He says that he hath taken them down again, for the man must not be 85 hanged till the next week.

Titus. But what says Jubiter, I ask thee?

Clown. Alas, sir, I know not Jubiter: I never drank with him in all my life.

Titus. Why, villain, art not thou the carrier? 90

Clown. Ay, of my pigeons, sir: nothing else.

Titus. Why, didst thou not come from Heaven?

Clown. From Heaven! alas, sir, I never came there. God forbid I should be so bold to press to Heaven in my young days. Why, I am going with my pigeons to 95 the tribunal plebs, to take up a matter of brawl betwixt my uncle and one of the Emperal's men.

Mar. Why, sir, that is as fit as can be to serve for your oration; and let him deliver the pigeons to the Emperor from you. 100

Titus. Tell me, can you deliver an oration to the Emperor with a grace?

Clown. Nay, truly, sir, I could never say grace in all my life.

Titus. Sirrah, come hither. Make no more ado 105
But give your pigeons to the Emperor.

117. **bravely:** with dash; finely.

118. **let me alone:** don't worry.

121. **For thou hast made it like an humble suppliant:** the syntax is difficult to fathom, but the point seems to be that the knife should be hidden so that the appearance of humble supplication is not destroyed.

IV. [iv.] Saturninus is already enraged at the annoyance caused by Titus' behavior when the Clown appears with his supplication. As soon as Saturninus has read it, he sentences the hapless messenger to be hanged. He is about to order Titus brought before him when a messenger announces the imminent approach of Lucius with an army of Goths, determined to destroy the city. Tamora convinces Saturninus that she will be able to persuade Titus to intercede with his son. She sends a message to Lucius requesting a parley at his father's house.

3. **overborne:** oppressed.

By me thou shalt have justice at his hands.
Hold, hold! Meanwhile here's money for thy charges.
Give me pen and ink.
Sirrah, can you with a grace deliver up a supplica- 110
tion?

 Clown. Ay, sir.

 Titus. Then here is a supplication for you. And
when you come to him, at the first approach you must
kneel; then kiss his foot; then deliver up your pigeons; 115
and then look for your reward. I'll be at hand, sir. See
you do it bravely.

 Clown. I warrant you, sir, let me alone.

 Titus. Sirrah, hast thou a knife? Come, let me see it.
Here, Marcus, fold it in the oration,   120
For thou hast made it like an humble suppliant.
And when thou hast given it to the Emperor,
Knock at my door and tell me what he says.

 Clown. God be with you, sir: I will.   *Exit.*

 Titus. Come, Marcus, let us go. Publius, follow me. 125
           Exeunt.

[Scene IV.   Rome.   Before the palace.]

*Enter Emperor [Saturninus] and Tamora, and her
two Sons, [Lords, and others;] the Emperor brings
 the arrows in his hand that Titus shot at him.*

 Sat. Why, lords, what wrongs are these! Was ever
  seen
An Emperor in Rome thus overborne,

4. **confronted:** opposed; **extent:** exercise.
5. **equal:** exact.
9. **even:** just.
12. **wreaks:** injuries.
19. **blazoning:** proclaiming.

Troubled, confronted thus, and for the extent
Of equal justice used in such contempt?　　　　　　5
My lords, you know, as know the mightful gods,
However these disturbers of our peace
Buzz in the people's ears, there nought hath passed
But even with law against the willful sons
Of old Andronicus. And what and if　　　　　　10
His sorrows have so overwhelmed his wits,
Shall we be thus afflicted in his wreaks,
His fits, his frenzy, and his bitterness?
And now he writes to Heaven for his redress.
See, here's to Jove, and this to Mercury;　　　　　15
This to Apollo; this to the god of war:
Sweet scrolls to fly about the streets of Rome!
What's this but libeling against the Senate
And blazoning our unjustice everywhere?
A goodly humor, is it not, my lords?　　　　　　20
As who would say in Rome no justice were.
But, if I live, his feigned ecstasies
Shall be no shelter to these outrages;
But he and his shall know that justice lives
In Saturninus' health; whom, if she sleep,　　　　25
He'll so awake as he in fury shall
Cut off the proud'st conspirator that lives.
　　Tam. My gracious lord, my lovely Saturnine,
Lord of my life, commander of my thoughts,
Calm thee and bear the faults of Titus' age,　　　30
The effects of sorrow for his valiant sons,
Whose loss hath pierced him deep and scarred his
　　　heart;

38. gloze: disguise (her true feelings with soothing words).

40. Thy lifeblood out: i.e., drawing out your lifeblood.

47. god-den: good evening.

50. must: shall.

52. brought up: raised.

And rather comfort his distressed plight
Than prosecute the meanest or the best   35
For these contempts. [*Aside*] Why, thus it shall be-
          come
High-witted Tamora to gloze with all.
But, Titus, I have touched thee to the quick,
Thy lifeblood out. If Aaron now be wise,   40
Then is all safe, the anchor in the port.

Enter Clown.

How now, good fellow! Wouldst thou speak with us?
    Clown. Yea, forsooth, and your mistress-ship be
emperial.
    Tam. Empress I am, but yonder sits the Emperor.   45
    Clown. 'Tis he. God and Saint Stephen give you
god-den. I have brought you a letter and a couple of
pigeons here.   [*Saturninus*] *reads the letter.*
    Sat. Go, take him away, and hang him presently!
    Clown. How much money must I have?   50
    Tam. Come, sirrah, you must be hanged.
    Clown. Hanged! By'r lady, then I have brought up
a neck to a fair end.   *Exit,* [*guarded*].
    Sat. Despiteful and intolerable wrongs!
Shall I endure this monstrous villainy?   55
I know from whence this same device proceeds.
May this be borne? As if his traitorous sons
That died by law for murder of our brother
Have by my means been butchered wrongfully!
Go, drag the villain hither by the hair: 60

61. **shape privilege:** provide immunity.

63. **Sly frantic:** i.e., pretended madman; **holpst:** helped.

67. **gathered head:** assembled an army.

68. **bent to the spoil:** determined on destruction.

69. **amain:** with all speed.

72. **Coriolanus:** a legendary Roman hero, whose unpopularity forced him into exile, where he joined Rome's enemies, the Volscians. The destruction of Rome under his leadership was finally averted when his wife and his mother appealed to his patriotism.

Nor age nor honor shall shape privilege.
For this proud mock I'll be thy slaughterman,
Sly frantic wretch, that holpst to make me great,
In hope thyself should govern Rome and me.

Enter Nuntius Aemilius.

What news with thee, Aemilius?   65
 Aem. Arm, my lords! Rome never had more cause.
The Goths have gathered head and with a power
Of high-resolved men, bent to the spoil,
They hither march amain, under conduct
Of Lucius, son to old Andronicus;   70
Who threats, in course of this revenge, to do
As much as ever Coriolanus did.
 Sat. Is warlike Lucius general of the Goths?
These tidings nip me, and I hang the head
As flowers with frost or grass beat down with storms.   75
Ay, now begins our sorrows to approach.
'Tis he the common people love so much:
Myself hath often heard them say,
When I have walked like a private man,
That Lucius' banishment was wrongfully,   80
And they have wished that Lucius were their
  Emperor.
 Tam. Why should you fear? Is not your city strong?
 Sat. Ay, but the citizens favor Lucius
And will revolt from me to succor him.   85
 Tam. King, be thy thoughts imperious like thy
  name.

89. **suffers:** permits.
90. **careful:** concerned.
92. **stint:** stop.
93. **giddy:** disloyal.
97. **honey stalks to sheep:** i.e., clover, from which sheep sometimes die of a surfeit.
98. **Whenas:** when.
102. **smooth:** flatter; coax.
111. **stand:** insist.
112. **pledge:** pawn.
115. **temper:** manipulate.

Is the sun dimmed that gnats do fly in it?
The eagle suffers little birds to sing
And is not careful what they mean thereby,   90
Knowing that with the shadow of his wings
He can at pleasure stint their melody.
Even so mayest thou the giddy men of Rome.
Then cheer thy spirit: for know, thou Emperor,
I will enchant the old Andronicus   95
With words more sweet, and yet more dangerous,
Than baits to fish or honey stalks to sheep,
Whenas the one is wounded with the bait,
The other rotted with delicious feed.
  Sat. But he will not entreat his son for us.   100
  Tam. If Tamora entreat him, then he will.
For I can smooth and fill his aged ears
With golden promises, that, were his heart
Almost impregnable, his old ears deaf,
Yet should both ear and heart obey my tongue.   105
[*To Aemilius*] Go thou before to be our ambassador.
Say that the Emperor requests a parley
Of warlike Lucius, and appoint the meeting
Even at his father's house, the old Andronicus.
  Sat. Aemilius, do this message honorably.   110
And if he stand on hostage for his safety,
Bid him demand what pledge will please him best.
  Aem. Your bidding shall I do effectually.   *Exit.*
  Tam. Now will I to that old Andronicus
And temper him with all the art I have,   115
To pluck proud Lucius from the warlike Goths.
And now, sweet Emperor, be blithe again

119. successantly: apparently a Shakespearean coinage, the exact sense of which is uncertain.

And bury all thy fear in my devices.

    Sat. Then go successantly and plead to him.

Exeunt.

TITUS
ANDRONICUS

ACT V

V. [i.] Lucius, encamped near Rome, receives from his soldiers the captured Aaron and his child. He is about to have Aaron hanged when the Moor dissuades him by promising to reveal the villainous deeds to which he has been a party, on condition that his child's life is spared. Lucius swears by his gods that he will spare the child, and Aaron reveals the names of the ravishers of Lavinia and the truth about Bassianus' murder. A messenger brings Saturninus' request for a parley, and Lucius agrees to the meeting on condition that hostages are left with Titus.

━━━━━━━━━━━━━━━━━━━━━━

1. **Approved:** experienced.
7. **scathe:** injury.
9. **slip:** offshoot; offspring.
14. **bold:** confident.

ACT V

[Scene I. Plains near Rome.]

Flourish. Enter Lucius with an army of Goths, with Drums and Soldiers.

Luc. Approved warriors, and my faithful friends,
I have received letters from great Rome
Which signifies what hate they bear their Emperor
And how desirous of our sight they are.
Therefore, great lords, be, as your titles witness,   5
Imperious and impatient of your wrongs;
And wherein Rome hath done you any scathe
Let him make treble satisfaction.
   1. Goth. Brave slip, sprung from the great Androni-
      cus,   10
Whose name was once our terror, now our comfort;
Whose high exploits and honorable deeds
Ingrateful Rome requites with foul contempt,
Be bold in us. We'll follow where thou leadst,
Like stinging bees in hottest summer's day,   15
Led by their master to the flowered fields,
And be avenged on cursed Tamora.
   Others. And as he saith, so say we all with him.

31. **lent:** given.
35. **rates:** scolds.
38. **hold:** regard.
44. **pearl:** cf. the proverb "A black man is a pearl in a fair woman's eye."

Luc. I humbly thank him, and I thank you all.
But who comes here, led by a lusty Goth?   20

*Enter a Goth, leading of Aaron with his Child in his
                        arms.*

2. *Goth.* Renowned Lucius, from our troops I
        strayed
To gaze upon a ruinous monastery;
And, as I earnestly did fix mine eye
Upon the wasted building, suddenly   25
I heard a child cry underneath a wall.
I made unto the noise, when soon I heard
The crying babe controlled with this discourse:
"Peace, tawny slave, half me and half thy dam!
Did not thy hue bewray whose brat thou art,   30
Had nature lent thee but thy mother's look,
Villain, thou mightst have been an emperor.
But where the bull and cow are both milk-white,
They never do beget a coal-black calf.
Peace, villain, peace!"—even thus he rates the babe—   35
"For I must bear thee to a trusty Goth,
Who, when he knows thou art the Empress' babe,
Will hold thee dearly for thy mother's sake."
With this, my weapon drawn, I rushed upon him,
Surprised him suddenly, and brought him hither,   40
To use as you think needful of the man.
    Luc. O worthy Goth, this is the incarnate devil
That robbed Andronicus of his good hand;
This is the pearl that pleased your Empress' eye;
And here's the base fruit of her burning lust.   45

46. **wall-eyed:** fiercely glaring.

49. **halter:** noose.

63. **nourished:** nursed; brought up.

69. **Ruthful:** piteous; **piteously:** there is a possible play on the sense, "devoutly," "religiously," sardonically used.

Say, wall-eyed slave, whither wouldst thou convey
This growing image of thy fiendlike face?
Why dost not speak? What, deaf? Not a word?
A halter, soldiers! Hang him on this tree,
And by his side his fruit of bastardy.   50

  Aar. Touch not the boy: he is of royal blood.

  Luc. Too like the sire for ever being good.
First hang the child, that he may see it sprawl;
A sight to vex the father's soul withal.
Get me a ladder.   55

    [*A ladder brought, which Aaron is made to ascend.*]

  Aar.   Lucius, save the child
And bear it from me to the Empress.
If thou do this, I'll show thee wondrous things
That highly may advantage thee to hear.
If thou wilt not, befall what may befall,   60
I'll speak no more, but vengeance rot you all!

  Luc. Say on: and, if it please me which thou speakst,
Thy child shall live, and I will see it nourished.

  Aar. And if it please thee! Why, assure thee, Lucius,
'Twill vex thy soul to hear what I shall speak;   65
For I must talk of murders, rapes, and massacres,
Acts of black night, abominable deeds,
Complots of mischief, treason, villainies
Ruthful to hear, yet piteously performed.
And this shall all be buried in my death   70
Unless thou swear to me my child shall live.

  Luc. Tell on thy mind: I say thy child shall live.

  Aar. Swear that he shall, and then I will begin.

  Luc. Who should I swear by? Thou believest no
    god: 75

78. **for:** because.

83. **idiot:** professional fool; **bauble:** a stick, usually surmounted by a conventional jester's face with a coxcomb.

92. **insatiate and luxurious:** insatiably lustful.

101–2. **Trim:** splendid, with a pun. Aaron speaks as though Lavinia had been barbered, and Lucius' adjective **barbarous** may acknowledge this.

104. **codding:** lascivious (cod: testicle).

A fool with his bauble. From Stephen Batman, *The Traveled Pilgrim* (1569).

That granted, how canst thou believe an oath?

   Aar. What if I do not? as, indeed, I do not:

Yet, for I know thou art religious

And hast a thing within thee called conscience,

With twenty popish tricks and ceremonies,   80

Which I have seen thee careful to observe,

Therefore I urge thy oath. [*Aside*] For that I know

An idiot holds his bauble for a god,

And keeps the oath which by that god he swears,

To that I'll urge him—Therefore thou shalt vow   85

By that same god, what god soe'er it be

That thou adorest and hast in reverence,

To save my boy, to nourish and bring him up,

Or else I will discover nought to thee.

   Luc. Even by my god I swear to thee I will.   90

   Aar. First know thou, I begot him on the Empress.

   Luc. Oh, most insatiate and luxurious woman!

   Aar. Tut, Lucius, this was but a deed of charity

To that which thou shalt hear of me anon.

'Twas her two sons that murdered Bassianus;   95

They cut thy sister's tongue and ravished her,

And cut her hands, and trimmed her as thou sawest.

   Luc. O detestable villain! Callst thou that trimming?

   Aar. Why, she was washed and cut and trimmed,

     and 'twas   100

Trim sport for them which had the doing of it.

   Luc. Oh, barbarous, beastly villains, like thyself!

   Aar. Indeed, I was their tutor to instruct them.

That codding spirit had they from their mother,

As sure a card as ever won the set.   105

That bloody mind, I think, they learned of me,

107. **true:** brave; **at head:** i.e., within reach of injury (a term from bull baiting).

109. **trained:** lured.

119. **pried me:** peered.

124. **swounded:** swooned.

128. **saying:** the proverbial saying "to blush like a black dog" was used to describe perfect insolence.

136. **forswear:** perjure.

As true a dog as ever fought at head.
Well, let my deeds be witness of my worth.
I trained thy brethren to that guileful hole
Where the dead corpse of Bàssianus lay.   110
I wrote the letter that thy father found,
And hid the gold within that letter mentioned,
Confederate with the Queen and her two sons—
And what not done that thou hast cause to rue,
Wherein I had no stroke of mischief in it?   115
I played the cheater for thy father's hand;
And, when I had it, drew myself apart
And almost broke my heart with extreme laughter.
I pried me through the crevice of a wall
When for his hand he had his two sons' heads,   120
Beheld his tears, and laughed so heartily
That both mine eyes were rainy like to his.
And, when I told the Empress of this sport,
She swounded almost at my pleasing tale
And for my tidings gave me twenty kisses.   125

   1. Goth. What, canst thou say all this and never
     blush?

   Aar. Ay, like a black dog, as the saying is.

   Luc. Art thou not sorry for these heinous deeds?

   Aar. Ay, that I had not done a thousand more.   130
Even now I curse the day—and yet, I think,
Few come within the compass of my curse—
Wherein I did not some notorious ill:
As kill a man, or else devise his death;
Ravish a maid, or plot the way to do it;   135
Accuse some innocent and forswear myself;
Set deadly enmity between two friends;

152. **presently:** instantly.

Make poor men's cattle break their necks;
Set fire on barns and haystacks in the night
And bid the owners quench them with their tears.   140
Oft have I digged up dead men from their graves
And set them upright at their dear friends' door,
Even when their sorrows almost was forgot;
And on their skins, as on the bark of trees,
Have with my knife carved in Roman letters,   145
"Let not your sorrow die, though I am dead."
Tut, I have done a thousand dreadful things
As willingly as one would kill a fly;
And nothing grieves me heartily indeed
But that I cannot do ten thousand more.   150
   Luc. Bring down the devil, for he must not die
So sweet a death as hanging presently.
   Aar. If there be devils, would I were a devil,
To live and burn in everlasting fire,
So I might have your company in hell   155
But to torment you with my bitter tongue!
   Luc. Sirs, stop his mouth, and let him speak no
    more.

         Enter Aemilius.

   3. Goth. My lord, there is a messenger from Rome
Desires to be admitted to your presence.   160
   Luc. Let him come near.
Welcome, Aemilius. What's the news from Rome?
   Aem. Lord Lucius, and you princes of the Goths,
The Roman Emperor greets you all by me;
And, for he understands you are in arms,   165

V. [ii.] Tamora plans to fool Titus, whom she believes mad, by assuming a disguise as Revenge, accompanied by her sons disguised as Rape and Murder. She hopes that this deception will enable her to trap Lucius. Titus recognizes the trio but pretends to accept their false identities. He agrees to provide a feast for Tamora and Saturninus when they come to his house, which "Revenge" promises to arrange. She slily suggests that Lucius be invited, and Titus sends Marcus to invite him. When Tamora departs to make arrangements, Titus has her sons bound. As Lavinia holds a basin to catch their blood, Titus cuts their throats, planning to have their blood and bones ground into a paste upon which he will feast their mother. He plans to serve the imperial couple himself.

⸻⸻⸻⸻⸻⸻

1. **sad habiliment:** somber clothing.
5. **keeps:** stays.
8. **confusion:** destruction.
11. **sad decrees:** grave decisions.
12. **study:** thought.

He craves a parley at your father's house,
Willing you to demand your hostages,
And they shall be immediately delivered.

   1. Goth. What says our General?

   Luc. Aemilius, let the Emperor give his pledges   **170**
Unto my father and my uncle Marcus,
And we will come. March away.

                          Flourish. Exeunt.

    [Scene II.   Rome.   Before Titus' house.]

   Enter Tamora and her two Sons, disguised.

   Tam. Thus, in this strange and sad habiliment,
I will encounter with Andronicus
And say I am Revenge, sent from below
To join with him and right his heinous wrongs.
Knock at his study, where they say he keeps   **5**
To ruminate strange plots of dire revenge:
Tell him Revenge is come to join with him
And work confusion on his enemies.

      They knock and Titus opens his study door.

   Titus. Who doth molest my contemplation?
Is it your trick to make me open the door,   **10**
That so my sad decrees may fly away
And all my study be to no effect?
You are deceived: for what I mean to do
See here in bloody lines I have set down;
And what is written shall be executed.   **15**

18. **give it that accord:** i.e., "suit the action to the word" (*Hamlet*, III.ii. 17–8). Appropriate gestures are made impossible by the loss of his hand.

19. **odds:** advantage.

25. **trenches:** deep facial lines.

26. **heavy:** miserable.

40. **couch:** hide.

Revenge personified. From Cesare Ripa, *Iconologie* (1677).

　　Tam. Titus, I am come to talk with thee.

　　Titus. No, not a word. How can I grace my talk,
Wanting a hand to give it that accord?
Thou hast the odds of me: therefore no more.

　　Tam. If thou didst know me, thou wouldst talk with　20
　　me.

　　Titus. I am not mad: I know thee well enough.
Witness this wretched stump, witness these crimson
　　lines;
Witness these trenches made by grief and care;　　25
Witness the tiring day and heavy night;
Witness all sorrow, that I know thee well
For our proud Empress, mighty Tamora!
Is not thy coming for my other hand?

　　Tam. Know, thou sad man, I am not Tamora:　　30
She is thy enemy, and I thy friend.
I am Revenge; sent from the infernal kingdom
To ease the gnawing vulture of thy mind
By working wreakful vengeance on thy foes.
Come down and welcome me to this world's light:　　35
Confer with me of murder and of death.
There's not a hollow cave or lurking place,
No vast obscurity or misty vale,
Where bloody murder or detested rape
Can couch for fear but I will find them out　　40
And in their ears tell them my dreadful name,
Revenge, which makes the foul offender quake.

　　Titus. Art thou Revenge? And art thou sent to me,
To be a torment to mine enemies?

　　Tam. I am. Therefore come down and welcome me.　　45

　　Titus. Do me some service ere I come to thee.

47. **Lo:** behold; **Rape and Murder:** Titus seems to have forgotten who they are in line 63, but perhaps this is part of his role as mock madman and is intended to disarm Tamora.

62. **ministers:** agents.

73. **closing with:** humoring.

74. **forge:** pretend.

Lo, by thy side where Rape and Murder stands;
Now give some 'surance that thou art Revenge,
Stab them, or tear them on thy chariot wheels;
And then I'll come and be thy wagoner   50
And whirl along with thee about the globes.
Provide thee two proper palfreys, black as jet,
To hale thy vengeful wagon swift away
And find out murderers in their guilty caves;
And when thy car is loaden with their heads   55
I will dismount and by thy wagon wheel
Trot like a servile footman all day long,
Even from Hyperion's rising in the East
Until his very downfall in the sea.
And day by day I'll do this heavy task,   60
So thou destroy Rapine and Murder there.
    Tam. These are my ministers and come with me.
    Titus. Are they thy ministers? What are they called?
    Tam. Rape and Murder: therefore called so
'Cause they take vengeance of such kind of men.   65
    Titus. Good Lord, how like the Empress' sons they
        are,
And you the Empress! But we worldly men
Have miserable, mad, mistaking eyes.
O sweet Revenge, now do I come to thee;   70
And, if one arm's embracement will content thee,
I will embrace thee in it by and by.   *Exit from above.*
    Tam. This closing with him fits his lunacy.
Whate'er I forge to feed his brain-sick humors
Do you uphold and maintain in your speeches,   75
For now he firmly takes me for Revenge;
And, being credulous in this mad thought,

80. **out of hand:** extempore.

81. **giddy:** inconstant.

88. **Well are you fitted:** i.e., you resemble them well.

90. **wags:** stirs.

93. **convenient:** appropriate.

I'll make him send for Lucius his son;
And, whilst I at a banquet hold him sure,
I'll find some cunning practice out of hand　　　80
To scatter and disperse the giddy Goths,
Or at the least make them his enemies.
See, here he comes, and I must ply my theme.

[Enter Titus, below.]

　Titus. Long have I been forlorn, and all for thee.
Welcome, dread Fury, to my woeful house.　　　85
Rapine and Murder, you are welcome too.
How like the Empress and her sons you are!
Well are you fitted, had you but a Moor.
Could not all hell afford you such a devil?
For well I wot the Empress never wags　　　90
But in her company there is a Moor;
And, would you represent our Queen aright,
It were convenient you had such a devil.
But welcome as you are. What shall we do?
　Tam. What wouldst thou have us do, Andronicus?　95
　Dem. Show me a murderer, I'll deal with him.
　Chir. Show me a villain that hath done a rape,
And I am sent to be revenged on him.
　Tam. Show me a thousand that hath done thee
　　wrong,　　　100
And I will be revenged on them all.
　Titus. Look round about the wicked streets of Rome,
And when thou findst a man that's like thyself,
Good Murder, stab him: he's a murderer.—

111. **up and down:** all in all; perfectly.
114. **lessoned:** instructed.

Go thou with him, and when it is thy hap   105
To find another that is like to thee,
Good Rapine, stab him: he's a ravisher.—
Go thou with them, and in the Emperor's court
There is a queen, attended by a Moor:
Well shalt thou know her by thine own proportion,   110
For up and down she doth resemble thee.
I pray thee, do on them some violent death:
They have been violent to me and mine.

   Tam. Well hast thou lessoned us: this shall we do.
But would it please thee, good Andronicus,   115
To send for Lucius, thy thrice valiant son,
Who leads toward Rome a band of warlike Goths,
And bid him come and banquet at thy house?
When he is here, even at thy solemn feast,
I will bring in the Empress and her sons,   120
The Emperor himself, and all thy foes;
And at thy mercy shall they stoop and kneel,
And on them shalt thou ease thy angry heart.
What says Andronicus to this device?

   Titus. Marcus, my brother! 'Tis sad Titus calls.   125

Enter Marcus.

Go, gentle Marcus, to thy nephew Lucius:
Thou shalt inquire him out among the Goths.
Bid him repair to me and bring with him
Some of the chiefest princes of the Goths.
Bid him encamp his soldiers where they are.   130
Tell him the Emperor and the Empress too
Feast at my house, and he shall feast with them.

140. cleave: cling.

144. governed: handled; **determined:** predetermined.

145. smooth: flatter.

149. o'erreach: outwit.

This do thou for my love, and so let him,
As he regards his aged father's life.

 Mar. This will I do, and soon return again. [*Exit.*] 135
 Tam. Now will I hence about thy business
And take my ministers along with me.

 Titus. Nay, nay, let Rape and Murder stay with me;
Or else I'll call my brother back again
And cleave to no revenge but Lucius. 140

 Tam. [*Aside to her sons*] What say you, boys? Will
  you abide with him,
Whiles I go tell my lord the Emperor
How I have governed our determined jest?
Yield to his humor, smooth and speak him fair, 145
And tarry with him till I turn again.

 Titus. [*Aside*] I knew them all, though they sup-
  posed me mad,
And will o'erreach them in their own devices—
A pair of cursed hellhounds and their dam! 150

 Dem. Madam, depart at pleasure: leave us here.
 Tam. Farewell, Andronicus. Revenge now goes
To lay a complot to betray thy foes.

 Titus. I know thou dost, and, sweet Revenge, farewell!   [*Exit Tamora.*] 155

 Chir. Tell us, old man, how shall we be employed?
 Titus. Tut, I have work enough for you to do.
Publius, come hither, Caius, and Valentine!

   [*Enter Publius, Caius, and Valentine.*]

 Pub. What is your will?
 Titus. Know you these two? 160

170. forbear: desist.

Pub. The Empress' sons, I take them, Chiron,
 Demetrius.

Titus. Fie, Publius, fie! Thou art too much deceived:
The one is Murder, and Rape is the other's name;
And therefore bind them, gentle Publius.   165
Caius and Valentine, lay hands on them.
Oft have you heard me wish for such an hour,
And now I find it: therefore bind them sure.
And stop their mouths, if they begin to cry.   [*Exit.*]
     [*Publius, etc., lay hold on Chiron and Demetrius.*]

Chir. Villains, forbear! We are the Empress' sons.   170

Pub. And therefore do we what we are commanded.
Stop close their mouths, let them not speak a word.
Is he sure bound? Look that you bind them fast.

*Enter Titus Andronicus with a knife and Lavinia with
a basin.*

Titus. Come, come, Lavinia: look, thy foes are
 bound.   175
Sirs, stop their mouths, let them not speak to me,
But let them hear what fearful words I utter.
O villains, Chiron and Demetrius!
Here stands the spring whom you have stained with
 mud,   180
This goodly summer with your winter mixed.
You killed her husband, and for that vile fault
Two of her brothers were condemned to death,
My hand cut off and made a merry jest;
Both her sweet hands, her tongue, and that more dear !ε
Than hands or tongue, her spotless chastity,

198. **coffin:** pastry shell; **rear:** make.

201. **increase:** offspring.

205. **Procne:** sister of Philomela and wife of Tereus, who fed him the flesh of his son to revenge his abuse of her sister.

211. **officious:** busy.

213. **stern:** cruel; **Centaurs' feast:** the marriage feast of Pirithous and Hippodameia, which turned into a bloody free-for-all when the Centaur Eurution abducted the bride.

Procne's feast for Tereus. From Gabriele Simeoni, *La vita et Metamorfoseo d'Ovidio* (1559).

Inhuman traitors, you constrained and forced.
What would you say if I should let you speak?
Villains, for shame you could not beg for grace.
Hark, wretches! how I mean to martyr you: 190
This one hand yet is left to cut your throats,
Whiles that Lavinia 'tween her stumps doth hold
The basin that receives your guilty blood.
You know your mother means to feast with me,
And calls herself Revenge, and thinks me mad.   195
Hark, villains! I will grind your bones to dust,
And with your blood and it I'll make a paste;
And of the paste a coffin I will rear,
And make two pasties of your shameful heads;
And bid that strumpet, your unhallowed dam,   200
Like to the Earth, swallow her own increase.
This is the feast that I have bid her to,
And this the banquet she shall surfeit on;
For worse than Philomel you used my daughter,
And worse than Procne I will be revenged.   205
And now prepare your throats. Lavinia, come,
Receive the blood: and when that they are dead,
Let me go grind their bones to powder small,
And with this hateful liquor temper it;
And in that paste let their vile heads be baked.   210
Come, come, be everyone officious
To make this banquet, which I wish may prove
More stern and bloody than the Centaurs' feast.

                                        He cuts their throats.

So!
Now bring them in, for I will play the cook,   215

216. against: before.

V. [iii.] Saturninus and Tamora duly arrive and are greeted by Titus, who then kills Lavinia, referring to Virginius' slaying of his daughter to spare her shame. He maintains that Demetrius and Chiron are really responsible for his daughter's death and, when asked where they are, points to the pie that Tamora has already tasted. He stabs Tamora, and Saturninus stabs him. Lucius, in turn, kills Saturninus. Marcus and Lucius address the Roman populace, relating the whole story of the injuries done their family. They ask the people to judge whether they have done wrong to avenge such villainies. The people hail Lucius as Emperor. Lucius condemns Aaron to be set in the earth and starved to death. Tamora's body is to be thrown to scavenging birds and beasts.

---

1. mind: will.

And see them ready against their mother comes.
     Exeunt, [bearing the dead bodies].

━━

[Scene III. Court of Titus' house. A banquet set out.]

Enter Lucius, Marcus, and the Goths, [with Aaron, prisoner].

 Luc. Uncle Marcus, since 'tis my father's mind
That I repair to Rome, I am content.
 Goth. And ours with thine, befall what fortune will.
 Luc. Good uncle, take you in this barbarous Moor,
This ravenous tiger, this accursed devil;   5
Let him receive no sust'nance, fetter him,
Till he be brought unto the Empress' face
For testimony of her foul proceedings.
And see the ambush of our friends be strong:
I fear the Emperor means no good to us.   10
 Aar. Some devil whisper curses in my ear,
And prompt me that my tongue may utter forth
The venomous malice of my swelling heart!
 Luc. Away, inhuman dog! unhallowed slave!
Sirs, help our uncle to convey him in,   15
     [Exeunt Goths, with Aaron.]
The trumpets show the Emperor is at hand.

Sound Trumpets. Enter Emperor [Saturninus] and Tamora, with [Aemilius,] Tribunes, [Senators,] and others.

17. **mo:** more.
18. **boots:** profits.
22. **careful:** solicitous; thoughtful.
24. **league and good:** good alliance.
30. **cheer:** fare.
37. **were:** would be.
39. **Virginius:** a centurion of the 5th century B.C., who killed his daughter Virginia before she could be ravished by her abductor, Appius Claudius. The word "because" may be an error for "before"; but perhaps the author wanted to cite an exact parallel to Lavinia's case and distorted the facts for his purpose.

Sat. What, hath the firmament mo suns than one?

Luc. What boots it thee to call thyself a sun?

Mar. Rome's Emperor, and nephew, break the
    parle: 20

These quarrels must be quietly debated.

The feast is ready which the careful Titus

Hath ordained to an honorable end,

For peace, for love, for league and good to Rome.

Please you, therefore, draw nigh and take your places. 25

    Sat. Marcus, we will.

        Trumpets sounding. [The Company sit at table.]

*Enter Titus, like a Cook, placing the dishes, and
Lavinia with a veil over her face, [young Lucius, and
        others].*

    Titus. Welcome, my gracious lord! Welcome, dread
    Queen!

Welcome, ye warlike Goths! Welcome, Lucius!

And welcome, all! Although the cheer be poor,   30

'Twill fill your stomachs: please you eat of it.

    Sat. Why art thou thus attired, Andronicus?

    Titus. Because I would be sure to have all well

To entertain your Highness and your empress.

    Tam. We are beholding to you, good Andronicus.   35

    Titus. And if your Highness knew my heart, you
    were.

My lord the Emperor, resolve me this:

Was it well done of rash Virginius

To slay his daughter with his own right hand,   40

Because she was enforced, stained, and deflowered?

44. **Because:** in order that.

47. **lively:** forceful; **warrant:** justification.

51. **unkind:** inhuman.

66. **daintily:** with pleasure, with a possible play on the sense "fastidiously."

69. **frantic:** lunatic.

Sat. It was, Andronicus.

Titus. Your reason, mighty lord?

Sat. Because the girl should not survive her shame
And by her presence still renew his sorrows.   45

   Titus. A reason mighty, strong, and effectual,
A pattern, precedent, and lively warrant
For me, most wretched, to perform the like.
Die, die, Lavinia, and thy shame with thee,
And with thy shame thy father's sorrow die!   50

                   He kills her.

Sat. What hast thou done, unnatural and unkind?

Titus. Killed her for whom my tears have made me
   blind.
I am as woeful as Virginius was
And have a thousand times more cause than he   55
To do this outrage, and it now is done.

   Sat. What, was she ravished? Tell who did the deed.

   Titus. Will't please you eat? Will't please your
   Highness feed?

   Tam. Why hast thou slain thine only daughter thus?   60

   Titus. Not I: 'twas Chiron and Demetrius.
They ravished her and cut away her tongue;
And they, 'twas they, that did her all this wrong.

   Sat. Go fetch them hither to us presently.

   Titus. Why, there they are both, baked in this pie,   65
Whereof their mother daintily hath fed,
Eating the flesh that she herself hath bred.
'Tis true, 'tis true: witness my knife's sharp point.

                   He stabs Tamora.

   Sat. Die, frantic wretch, for this accursed deed!

                   [*Kills Titus.*]

71. **meed:** desert.

73. **severed:** dispersed.

76. **mutual:** common.

78. **bane:** destruction.

82. **frosty signs:** gray hairs; **chaps of age:** aged cheeks.

85. **erst:** once.

86. **ancestor:** Aeneas.

90. **subtle:** crafty.

91. **Sinon:** the Greek who persuaded the Trojans to take in the horse filled with Greek soldiers, so that the Greeks were able to capture the city.

93. **civil:** domestic; the result of civil war.

94. **compact:** composed.

Sinon views Troy complacently. From Geoffrey Whitney, *A Choice of Emblems* (1586).

Luc. Can the son's eye behold his father bleed?   70
There's meed for meed, death for a deadly deed!
   [*Kills Saturninus. A great tumult. Lucius, Marcus,*
            and others go up into the balcony.]
  Mar. You sad-faced men, people and sons of Rome,
By uproars severed, as a flight of fowl
Scattered by winds and high tempestuous gusts,
Oh, let me teach you how to knit again   75
This scattered corn into one mutual sheaf,
These broken limbs again into one body;
Lest Rome herself be bane unto herself,
And she whom mighty kingdoms curtsy to,
Like a forlorn and desperate castaway,   80
Do shameful execution on herself.
But if my frosty signs and chaps of age,
Grave witnesses of true experience,
Cannot induce you to attend my words,
[*To Lucius*] Speak, Rome's dear friend, as erst our   85
    ancestor,
When with his solemn tongue he did discourse
To lovesick Dido's sad attending ear
The story of that baleful burning night
When subtle Greeks surprised King Priam's Troy: 90
Tell us what Sinon hath bewitched our ears,
Or who hath brought the fatal engine in
That gives our Troy, our Rome, the civil wound.
My heart is not compact of flint nor steel;
Nor can I utter all our bitter grief,   95
But floods of tears will drown my oratory
And break my utt'rance, even in the time
When it should move ye to attend me most

102. **auditory:** audience.
106. **fell faults:** cruel crimes.
107. **cozened:** cheated.
119. **vaunter:** boaster.
124. **men praise themselves:** a proverbial idea.

And force you to commiseration.
Here's Rome's young captain, let him tell the tale: 100
While I stand by and weep to hear him speak.

   Luc. Then, gracious auditory, be it known to you
That Chiron and the damned Demetrius
Were they that murdered our emperor's brother;
And they it were that ravished our sister.   105
For their fell faults our brothers were beheaded,
Our father's tears despised, and basely cozened
Of that true hand that fought Rome's quarrel out
And sent her enemies unto the grave.
Lastly, myself unkindly banished,   110
The gates shut on me, and turned weeping out,
To beg relief among Rome's enemies;
Who drowned their enmity in my true tears,
And oped their arms to embrace me as a friend.
I am the turned-forth, be it known to you,   115
That have preserved her welfare in my blood
And from her bosom took the enemy's point,
Sheathing the steel in my advent'rous body.
Alas, you know I am no vaunter, I!
My scars can witness, dumb although they are,   120
That my report is just and full of truth.
But, soft! methinks I do digress too much,
Citing my worthless praise. Oh, pardon me,
For when no friends are by, men praise themselves.

   Mar. Now is my turn to speak. Behold the child: 125
   [*Pointing to the Child in the arms of an Attendant.*]
Of this was Tamora delivered,
The issue of an irreligious Moor,
Chief architect and plotter of these woes.

140. **mutual closure:** common finish.

155. **give me aim:** leave me alone; allow me a moment's grace.

The villain is alive in Titus' house,
Damned as he is, to witness this is true.   130
Now judge what cause had Titus to revenge
These wrongs unspeakable, past patience,
Or more than any living man could bear.
Now have you heard the truth, what say you, Romans?
Have we done aught amiss, show us wherein,   135
And, from the place where you behold us pleading,
The poor remainder of Andronici
Will, hand in hand, all headlong hurl ourselves
And on the ragged stones beat forth our souls,
And make a mutual closure of our house.   140
Speak, Romans, speak, and if you say we shall,
Lo, hand in hand, Lucius and I will fall.

    Aem. Come, come, thou reverend man of Rome,
And bring our emperor gently in thy hand,
Lucius our emperor, for well I know   145
The common voice do cry it shall be so.

    Mar. Lucius, all hail, Rome's royal emperor!
Go, go into old Titus' sorrowful house,
                              [To Attendants.]
And hither hale that misbelieving Moor
To be adjudged some direful slaught'ring death,   150
As punishment for his most wicked life.
                         [Exeunt Attendants]
        [Lucius, Marcus, and the others descend.]
Lucius, all hail, Rome's gracious governor!

    Luc. Thanks, gentle Romans. May I govern so
To heal Rome's harms and wipe away her woe!
But, gentle people, give me aim awhile,   155
For nature puts me to a heavy task.

157. **aloof:** apart.
158. **obsequious:** appropriate to funeral obsequies.
163. **tenders:** offers.

Stand all aloof, but, uncle, draw you near
To shed obsequious tears upon this trunk.
Oh, take this warm kiss on thy pale cold lips,

[Kissing Titus.]

These sorrowful drops upon thy bloodstained face,   160
The last true duties of thy noble son!

   Mar. Tear for tear and loving kiss for kiss
Thy brother Marcus tenders on thy lips.
Oh, were the sum of these that I should pay
Countless and infinite, yet would I pay them!   165

   Luc. Come hither, boy: come, come, and learn of
     us
To melt in showers. Thy grandsire loved thee well.
Many a time he danced thee on his knee,
Sung thee asleep, his loving breast thy pillow.   170
Many a story hath he told to thee,
And bid thee bear his pretty tales in mind
And talk of them when he was dead and gone.

   Mar. How many thousand times hath these poor
     lips,   175
When they were living, warmed themselves on thine!
O, now, sweet boy, give them their latest kiss.
Bid him farewell; commit him to the grave;
Do him that kindness, and take leave of him.

   Boy. O grandsire, grandsire! ev'n with all my heart   180
Would I were dead, so you did live again!
O Lord, I cannot speak to him for weeping;
My tears will choke me, if I ope my mouth.

[Enter Attendants with Aaron.]

   Rom. You sad Andronici, have done with woes.

211–14. **See . . . ruinate:** not in the First Quarto but added in the Second Quarto and Folio texts.

213. **order well:** set well in order; make orderly arrangements in.

Give sentence on this execrable wretch   185
That hath been breeder of these dire events.
　　Luc. Set him breast-deep in earth and famish him;
There let him stand and rave and cry for food.
If any one relieves or pities him,
For the offense he dies. This is our doom.   190
Some stay to see him fastened in the earth.
　　Aar. Ah, why should wrath be mute and fury
　　　dumb?
I am no baby, I, that with base prayers
I should repent the evils I have done.   195
Ten thousand worse than ever yet I did
Would I perform, if I might have my will.
If one good deed in all my life I did,
I do repent it from my very soul.
　　Luc. Some loving friends convey the Emperor   200
　　　hence
And give him burial in his father's grave.
My father and Lavinia shall forthwith
Be closed in our household's monument.
As for that ravenous tiger, Tamora,   205
No funeral rite, nor man in mourning weed,
No mournful bell shall ring her burial;
But throw her forth to beasts and birds of prey.
Her life was beastly and devoid of pity,
And, being dead, let birds on her take pity.   210
[See justice done on Aaron, that damned Moor,
By whom our heavy haps had their beginning.
Then, afterwards, to order well the state
That like events may ne'er it ruinate.]
　　　　　　　　　　　　　　　　Exeunt.

KEY TO

Famous Lines

These words are razors to my wounded heart.
                    [*Titus*—I. i. 328]

He lives in fame that died in virtue's cause.
                    [*Andronici*—I. i. 410]

She is a woman, therefore may be wooed;
She is a woman, therefore may be won.
                    [*Demetrius*—II. i. 89–90]

What you cannot as you would achieve,
You must perforce accomplish as you may.
                    [*Aaron*—II. i. 118–19]

The hunt is up, the morn is bright and gay,
The fields are fragrant, and the woods are green.
                    [*Titus*—II. ii. 1–2]

The birds chant melody on every bush;
The snake lies rolled in the cheerful sun;
The green leaves quiver with the cooling wind
And make a chequered shadow on the ground.
                    [*Tamora*—II. iii. 12–5]

What fool hath added water to the sea,
Or brought a fagot to bright-burning Troy?
                    [*Titus*—III. i. 69–70]